ABUSE OF WOMEN
IN
INDIAN CHRISTIAN FAMILIES

Preventive Role of Church and Theological Institutions

ABUSE OF WOMEN
IN
INDIAN CHRISTIAN FAMILIES

Preventive Role of Church and Theological Institutions

Thomas Varghese

2018

Abuse of Women in Indian Christian Families: *Preventive Role of Church and Theological Institutions* — Published by the Rev. Dr. Ashish Amos of the Indian Society for Promoting Christian Knowledge (ISPCK), Post Box 1585, 1654, Madarsa Road, Kashmere Gate, Delhi-110006 under its Women's Empowerment Programme (WEP-41).

© Author, 2013
Revised and Enlarged Edition, 2018

ISBN: 978-81-8465-678-7

Cover picture credit: pngtree.com

Laser typeset by

ISPCK, Post Box 1585, 1654, Madarsa Road, Kashmere Gate, Delhi-110006
• *Tel:* 23866323/22

e-mail: ashish@ispck.org.in • ella@ispck.org.in
website: www.ispck.org.in

This book is affectionately dedicated to

My beloved parents late Mrs. Kunjamma Thomas

and Mr. K. P. Thomas, who taught me the Christian values,

guided me to accept his calling in my life, sustained me

in his ministry and stood with me through life's challenges

till their last breath.

Contents

Acknowledgments

"Gratitude is the fairest blossom which springs from the soul."

Henry W Beecher

I believe that the Lord gave me a longing to write, the ability to publish this book and has preserved me in this project. I am grateful to the Lord Almighty for all those He sent to help, teach, reshape, encourage and above all to pray for me.

- I express my sincere gratitude to Dr. Vivian Churness for writing '*foreword*' for the second edition after thoroughly going through the entire manuscript. She is a retired faculty member of the University of Southern California, Department of Nursing in USA, and a former missionary-nurse in South India; she has co-authored four textbooks for nurses in India.

- I am indebted to South Asia Institute of Advanced Christian Studies (SAIACS) where I could complete D. Min successfully and later publish my D. Min dissertation on "Abuse of women in Christian families- Role of clergy, church and theological institutions." as a book in the year 2013. I would remiss not to mention the names of these special people namely Dr. Beulah Wood, and (late) Dr. G. Isaiah my mentors in D. Min programme.

- I express my sincere gratitude to Dr. Ian Payne, former Principal of SAIACS for writing the *foreword* and to June Hedlund and Susheela Koshi, who *proof read* the First edition.

- I also want to thank the ISPCK's team who made this book available for the public.

- Without the comments received from the readers and critics I would not have attempted to revise this book. Thank you all.

- Lastly, thanks go to my beloved wife Lalitha, my sons Anish and Vivin and their spouses Blessy and Smitha who have untiringly given their time and constantly encouraged me throughout the period involved in both the editions. Special mention about my three year old grandson Reuben whose curiosity had no ends while I was continuously working on my laptop.

What really makes a book are the people. In addition to relying on each other, the faithfulness and steadfast love of our Lord Almighty has enabled me to make my dream a reality this day. My prayer is that this book will honour the God Almighty, prevent abuse and encourage the hurt.

I remember where the Lord found me; any credit must go to Him alone.

Foreword

Media reporting has increased awareness of the abuse of women not only in India, but in the United States and other countries as well. A topic no one likes to talk about, it is now openly being addressed globally.

The Rev. Dr. Thomas Varghese writes about the abuse of women in India. Once I started reading this book it was hard to put it down. Based on his extensive research, the author tells the stories of women and girls in Indian society who have experienced many forms of abuse. He also gives accounts of abuse of women recorded in both the Old and New Testaments of the Bible. Human nature has not changed.

Because Jesus respected and honoured women, one would think that abuse of women does not occur in the Christian Church, but that is not the case. After interviewing many women and pastors in South India, Dr. Varghese found that abuse does occur and, in most instances, pastors and others do not intervene. Women suffer silently and needlessly, thinking nothing can be done. The book concludes with suggestions of how pastors and congregations can prevent and reduce abuse of women.

Pastors, social workers, and health professionals will find this book to be interesting reading. As they read the stories of women who have experience abuse, and of pastors who tried to help, or did not help, they will gain insight as to how they can assist others in similar situations.

They will also be better equipped to educate men and women of the need for mutual respect and honour.

Vivian Churness RN, PhD
Retd. Faculty, University of Southern California
June 2018

Preface

I am delighted to write the second edition of this book - the journey thus far-along my study, meditation and reflections about abuse of women in Christian families. I am happy to write the preface for the revised edition of my book with a deep sense of achievement and for God's faithfulness, wisdom, health and perseverance. God led me to revise and publish it after 5 years.

The data collected from the women who are hurt was unbelievable; to add to this, the sensationalism and publicity directed towards abuse of women have reached a dramatic level rocking our country at every level in recent years. From infants, children, young & older women - all are being abused by the father, brother, family members, friends, clergy, pastors, God men, neighbours, unknown persons or even street walkers. This is happening everywhere, and Christian families are no exception from this incidence. However, the author has focussed only about Christian families.

It is indeed alarming that the problem of abuse is very much in existence in Christian families, this reality and acceptance can find solution for its prevention. My main concern is to create awareness about the extent of this problem and to reiterate the valuable role and accountability of clergy, church and the theological colleges to prevent, reduce or eliminate the abuse of women in Christian families.

The socio-cultural perspectives of the abuse of Christian women are elaborated in this book. The author thoroughly studied and analyzed the Biblical view on the abuse of women and focused on the expected role of the clergy, and church in the prevention, reduction or the elimination of abuse of women, especially in married women. The data was based on the responses from married Christian women; the responses given by clergy from different denominations which were analyzed and interpreted.

This book is a revised edition in every means. Obviously there is continuity with previous work, but the structure, content and some of the thoughts are additional or modified. There are sentences and paragraphs which I have revised to improve the inadequate expression, to give more clarity in thoughts, words and sentences, in growing knowledge and smooth flow of transition. Most of the additions, correction and improvements have been made by referring books, latest data and of course from the comments received from the readers and critics of the first edition. Every principles set forth in the following pages is supported by Biblical precedent (reference).

It is my sincere prayer and hope that the book will be an authentic life changing agent in family, church, and society at large and in our own country, through the ministry of reconciliation. May it increase our commitment and healing touch to our own God given family. Let this book be useful in church, women's groups, youth group, cell groups, and families to develop a personal commitment and foster an abiding relationship with Jesus Christ.

It is noteworthy to say that this book is referred by many nursing schools and colleges for teaching few chapters in 'Sociology' and by very many others who are working with those who are hurt.

May the little seeds of thought written in this book sprout, warmed by the sunlight of knowledge and wisdom, watered by the wise words of instruction and nurtured by the loving acts of kindness.

All praise and glory to God the Almighty who grants me wisdom, creativity, time, abundant grace, mercy and love to complete this book He has assigned me to do in His time.

Rev. Dr. Thomas Varghese (Ivanachen)
June 2018

Chapter 1

Introduction

In the early days, the author has witnessed, in his own neighbourhood, the physical abuse of a woman by her husband where his parents had to intervene quite often. His father was acquainted with the clergy who intervened and restored peace in the family eventually. The entire parish was praying for the couple. After ordination, the author had to get involved with a family where the woman next door was frequently abused by her husband. The author attempted to resolve the problem. The parish as well as the affected family didn't appreciate the idea of him getting involved. Their argument was on why the author wants to get involved in the personal matter. Isn't it common in most of the families? Even if there is a severe fight, involvement by clergy will invite trouble in the church. However, I could help the family at last. Getting involved can adversely affect the image, friendship or personality of the clergy. The main reason for selecting the topic for this book stems from this incident and the vivid memories of the earlier period in the author's life.

Why is the abuse of women in Christian families in India a serious concern? Why should it be addressed by the church or clergy? This is an ongoing evil affair in every society, especially in our Indian society. We need to find a solution for this ongoing problem of abuse of women by their own husbands, so that they can live together peacefully and amicably as a family for the glory of God. Abuse by men is very much present in our Indian society and in the church. The media enlightens us on women committing suicide, burns cases, and heavy bruises due to such abuse. Many have witnessed the physical abuse of women because it is so visible. But there are many types of abuse which are not seen- like spiritual, emotional, social, and financial. Due to globalization, media dissemination or broadcasting and advocacy, a few cases of women's abuse have been brought to the public eye and Indian Christian women have experienced them all.

Domestic abuse or violence means the use or threat of physical abuse or violence to control a family member or intimate partner. In other words, it is the use of inhuman force to control a partner who should be treated with great respect in dignity and love.

Abuse or fear of abuse can limit a person's potential efficiency and capacity in her work, at home and the smooth and efficient functioning of family life which affects the physical, emotional, social and spiritual health of a person. It has been recognized as a violation of the basic human rights of women and of their exercise of fundamental freedom. It can inhibit one's capacity to contribute to quality work, success in life, or to plan and make choices in an effective manner. In some families, the children constantly witness the abuse. Even if the abuse takes place within the household, it affects women in all spheres of their lives. It affects autonomy, productivity, capacity, capability and quality of daily life and living. In today's scenario abuse of women is no longer a private matter but a matter of great concern for society. Therefore the clergy and church have to take this issue very seriously. Since the family is the basic unit of any society, healthy families are needed to constitute a strong society and also 'spiritually alive' homes and churches. According to the Biblical view, Christian traditions and the family are sacred because it is God designed and God ordained.

The Biblical concept of a God ordained marriage does not give any room for abuse of women in Christian marriage. God's intention of marriage is for companionship and fellowship and not for abuse. The constant abuse of women leads to insecurity or instability in marriage, disharmony at home, and makes the wife appear inefficient, ineffective and incompetent in her home, her church and society.

Accordingly the abuse of women affects the harmony of the entire family and church directly or indirectly. Knowingly or unknowingly the majority of clergy and the church turn a blind eye to this very important and crucial issue of confirming or denying the fact of abuse. Abuse against any human being is wrong ethically and cannot be justified. It is not Biblical nor it is human. Therefore God does not like or appreciate this kind of inhuman behaviour. The Bible does not encourage or give any room for unnecessary, unethical and unbiblical male domination in any manner at any time or anywhere. God has given authority for man and woman, "to rule over the fish of the sea and the birds of the air and over every living creature that moves on the ground" (Genesis 1:28). Dr. Richard S. Hess, in closely investigating the first three chapters of the book of Genesis, makes the case that both male and female are created in God's image. What is essential to this idea of 'image bearing' is the dominion that men and women are given over the earth. He writes, "There is nothing in this first chapter to suggest anything other than an equality of male and female created together in the image of God."[1] "The purpose of the sequential creation of Adam and then Eve in Genesis 2 is to show the need they have for each other and the unity (one-flesh) of their relationship."[2] Hess observes that man (male and female) is given joint responsibility over all his creation, but nowhere is man given authority over woman. "Man is given authority over the garden; nowhere is man given authority over woman. They are co-rulers, as joint heirs and image bearers of God."[3]

In the 'Parable of the Good Samaritan,' Jesus emphasizes our responsibility to demonstrate care, concern, love, and sympathy for the victim helplessly lying on the road. He also stresses our social and spiritual responsibility in preventing violence and of caring for the victim. Jesus said in John 10:10, 'I came that you may have life, and have it abundantly." The Word of God condemns the violent behavioural pattern of controlling and encourages peaceful living. The Bible exhorts us towards loving and responsible relationships between members of the family, with each honouring and providing for the needs of the other.

The Old Testament contains incidents of violent attitudes against women. In Genesis 34, Shechem, the son of Hamor sexually abused Dinah, the daughter of Leah and Jacob (v2). In 2 Samuel 13:14 Amnon physically and sexually assaulted Tamar. In Judges 19, the Levite's concubine was physically and sexually abused (v.25). These examples give rise to the question whether the Bible teaches silence for women during the abuse. In Esther 1, we see how Queen Vashti faces social and psychological violence. Vashti and Esther, remind us that some women have resisted male domination and violence.

In the New Testament, the persistent widow in the parable in Luke 18: 2 was socially abused. This widow is helpless and vulnerable because she had no family members to support her or intercede in her matter. The judge was unconcerned or indifferent to her needs. In John 8:1-8 we see the woman who was caught in adultery. The accusers brought only one offender instead of both. The intention of the accusers was to abuse her physically, socially and psychologically in front of the large crowd. Jesus' response to the accusers is amazing, 'if any one of you is without sin, let him be the first to throw a stone at her." (v7). Jesus condemned and hated the sin; but had compassion not only for women but for all humanity. The story of the woman faced with discrimination is recorded in three of the four gospels (Matthew 26:6-13; Mark 14:3-9; John 12:1-7). This must have been an important event. Matthew and Mark do not mention the name of the woman, probably because women were unimportant in those days. Only John mentions her name. The story has given three progressions of the woman's actions. Firstly she breaks into a state of affairs, secondly she breaks the alabaster jar, and thirdly she breaks out of an aggressively biased situation. This woman faced social, physical and psychological abuse from the people who were gathered there and especially from the disciples. Jesus set a pattern for his disciples and others about liberating the oppressed and also how to empower the liberated woman.

Abuse of women is prevalent, and widespread in every society, every culture and every church all over the world. It exists irrespective of educational, financial or social status, age, religion or race. The people who are most frequently and commonly abused in our Indian society are women, children, the elderly, mentally challenged, and the differently- abled. In other words, the weaker sections are mostly attacked. The embarrassment, humiliation and the fear that women feel about abuse or violence too often discourage them from bringing this issue to the light or sharing it with others. A woman's point of view on abuse differs from individual to individual. The woman, who prefers to remain silent or keep hiding, either does not have enough courage to say it publicly or decides to suffer quietly, accepting it as her fate. Some women are willing to come forward fearlessly and say they are abused. However the majority of laymen and clergy think that the rate of abuse of women in Indian Christian families by their husbands is negligible, insignificant, or unimportant. In fact some of the churches and clergy deny the fact of the existence of abuse of married women in their respective parishes or in Christian families. Only when clergy and the church at large accept the existence of abuse and realize their responsibilities, can precautionary measures be taken more effectively and systematically.

Clergy have a role in preventing abuse. The clergy may not be adequately trained or prepared to handle the situation of abuse. With pastoral care a positive attitude can be inculcated in the life of the husband who is abusing the wife. The clergy's support will make it possible for the victim and victimizer to improve their interpersonal relationship and sustain the same.

A detailed study was conducted to ascertain the level, type and the seriousness of the abuse faced by women from their husbands in Christian families in India and the preparedness of clergy to minister in these situations in dealing with this issue. Based on Biblical doctrine, theological perspectives, social and cultural outlook, and the outcome of the study, appropriate recommendations are made for clergy and laity in preventing the abuse of women.

There were limitations for this study. Firstly, individual, cultural, linguistic, educational, and economic differences can normally lead to biased responses affecting the study. Secondly, due to personal bias, ego and the stigma attached, there can be reservations or uncertainties in giving proper and adequate answers with integrity. Thirdly, since it is a sensitive issue, a full-fledged study may not be possible.

The methodology used for the study was a combination of several modes of research. Taking into consideration the nature, purpose and scope of the study, a multi-disciplinary approach is needed to deal with this subject. The following approaches are, therefore, thoughtfully considered and selected to achieve the objectives in writing this book. In order to obtain an idea of the prevalence of abuse of women, a qualitative and quantitative method of research was used for this study. In order to gain insights into the topic, comprehensive library research was done. The scripture and its commentaries were meticulously studied. In addition to books, articles related to the topic from newspapers, periodicals and journals were studied at length. Information through the internet was also greatly useful for this study.

The questionnaire was one of the most important methods used for data collection. It was administered directly by the author or sent by post and e-mail. The respondents gave answers without the unnecessary intervention of the author. The questionnaire method is applicable only to educated people; for others interviews were conducted. In order to obtain authentic information for the research questions for this book, one hundred questionnaires each for married women and clergy were prepared in English language. During the process of preparing the questionnaire, the author held discussions and interviews with clergy of different denominations, a few leaders from women's help groups (both government and non-government organizations), and a few women who have experienced abuse and a few friends. The questions were prepared based on the library research, interviews and the above mentioned focus group discussions. Consequently the questions were corrected, revised and re-worded. Questionnaires were sent by e-mail and by ordinary post also.

Interviews were conducted for those unable to read or write or afraid to write it down as it was a written proof. Personal or face to face interviews were conducted at a time and place (home, working place, church, friend's home) convenient to the respondents. Non-personal interviews were conducted over the telephone and the responses were recorded immediately. Each of the interviews took around two hours. Interviewers were instructed well in advance to change the subject of discussion, if the interview was interrupted by anyone. In-depth interviews were conducted of the respondents who were willing to talk and report about the experience of the abuse, flow of events and their suggestion to prevent or reduce abuse. This was not possible with the non-personal interviews. The clergy, who were personally interviewed, discussed various issues in-depth with regard to abuse of women.

This study would have not been possible without the assistance of 'data collectors' who worked hard and sometimes agonized and shared the invisible and silent pain of many women who they met and interviewed. Though the data collectors had previous experience in field surveys, they were given intensive training for two days. The training was given in the area of the concept of gender, abuse of women, ethical standards in collecting the data and on interview techniques. They had hands-on practical training in using the questionnaire and going over each of the questions to ensure that they understood the terminology used therein. Discussions were held in order to acquaint them with the objectives of the study, questionnaire and interview schedule. They were also prepared to translate the questionnaire according to the convenience of the respondents. The interviewers were prepared to ask questions in the correct sequence, exactly as they appeared on the questionnaire. The data collectors were always made to travel in pairs (one male and one female) for their safety and protection, convenience and unbiased study. They were provided with mobile phones, laptops and transportation arrangements were made. The data collected was sent to the author through e-mail wherever internet facilities were available; otherwise it was handed over personally during the regular weekly meetings. The emotional needs of the interviewers were also taken into serious consideration. The data collectors met the author regularly; at times meetings were rescheduled to discuss their feelings, how it was affecting them and also to be briefed about the progress made by them. They could contact the author over the phone at any time of the day or night to clear their doubts and for any guidance. The author benefited enormously from the information obtained through these interviews. The author held a series of discussions with the data collectors in order to acquaint them with the objectives of the study, questionnaire and interview schedule. They were also equipped to translate the questionnaire according to the convenience of the respondents due to the language barrier of some respondents.

As the research topic is a sensitive issue, the respondents were selected by keeping the following criteria set by the author: They were married Christian women, who were willing to co-operate with the study, were reliable, and willing to share or discuss the issue of abuse without any exaggeration. This study is limited to abuse of women by her spouse in Indian Christian families. The study is limited to one hundred married women and one hundred clergymen. Of the one hundred married Indian Christian women who were the subject of this study, sixty five respondents were personally interviewed by the data collectors and thirty five respondents completed the questionnaire. One hundred clergy were included in the study; the data collectors personally interviewed twenty of them.

Definitions of main Concepts

Several terms and concepts are central and should be briefly explained to understand the concept of abuse of women in Indian Christian families in India. The author developed a number of easy and simple definitions for the different forms of abuse for the layman to understand. For this book terminologies like abuse, violence, and harassment are synonymous.

Abuse "is a normal professional term for physical, sexual, or emotional violence towards another. This term has also been used in relation to addictions that are damaging to the person."[4]

Cultural abuse is an attempt to attack particularly in the cultural identity to inflict suffering, or as a means of control.

Domestic abuse or violence "is a pattern of assault and coercive behavior, including physical, sexual, and psychological attacks as well as economic coercion, which adults or adolescents use against their intimate partners or vulnerable family members."[5]

Emotional abuse is an attempt to control another individual by using emotions as a weapon of his / her choice.

Financial abuse includes unrealistic dowry demands, taking complete control over wife's finances, constant demands for financial assistance; depriving financial needs of wife, economic blackmail, denial of property rights, and denial of access to education or employment.

Physical abuse includes intentional and deliberate use of physical force causing, disability, injury, harm or even death. It includes hair pulling, biting, poking, burning, vigorous shaking, slapping, kicking, pushing, attempting to strangle, use of restraints, scratching, shoving, throwing, hitting with objects causing bruises, cuts, and danger to life.

Psychological abuse includes humiliation, intimidation, causing embarrassment in front of others, doubts or suspicion, dishonouring, victimizing, emotional deprivation, lack of affection and failure to protect, controlling activities, withholding information, not taking care of the wife during illness and isolating the victim from the family.

Sexual abuse includes forced sexual activity, forcing perverted or deviate sex, denial of regular normal sexual relationship, and sadistic behaviour.

Social abuse means to isolate, or restrict the wife going out from the home, meeting friends, attending functions or parties, prohibiting access to transport, telephone and media like television, internet, and newspaper.

Spiritual abuse is the use of spiritual or religious beliefs, customs and practices to control and dominate another, not permitting to practice religion or rituals, forcing religious belief, compelling religious conversion, forcing practicing sorcery and witch craft.

Structural abuse is the process by which an individual is dealt with unfairly by a system of harm in ways that the person cannot protect themselves against, cannot deal with, cannot break out of, cannot mobilize against, cannot seek justice for, cannot redress, cannot avoid, cannot reverse and cannot change.

Verbal abuse includes using bad or hurting words or language in the presence or absence of others; scolding, yelling, screaming, murmuring, grumbling, expressing anger, threats to harm, and causing uneasiness.

Church is the gathering of all Christians regarded as a spiritual body.

Clergy refer to person ordained for religious duties or church leaders. In this study, the word clergy, pastor or priest will be used interchangeably.

Gender means the combination of socially and culturally constructed differences between women and men.

Harassment is the act of systematic and or continued unwanted and annoying actions of one party or a group, including threats and demands. It simply means that the behavior which annoys or upsets a person for a short or long period depends upon the genuineness of the issue.

Ill-treatment means to treat unkindly or harshly.

Lay person refers to non-clergy, a member of the local congregation.

Marriage is the state of being united to a person of the opposite sex as husband or wife in a consensual and contractual relationship, recognized by law of the land and in accordance with Biblical standards.

Patriarchy means society controlled by men in general.

Respondent refers to an individual who provided answers, verbally or non-verbally, for this study.

Violence against women is defined as "any act of gender based violence that results in, or is likely to result in physical, sexual, or psychological harm or suffering to women, including threats of such acts, coercion or arbitrary deprivation of liberty, whether occurring in public or private life."[6]

Spouse is a person's partner in marriage.

Victim is the woman who finds herself powerless in the whole situation of abuse.

Woman is the 'bone of his bone' and 'flesh of his flesh' of man. In Hebrew language 'bone of bone' means counterpart, perfect partner, completer of me, from me.

Endnotes

[1] Richard S. Hess, "Equality With and Without Innocence: Genesis 1-3," Discovering Biblical Equality: Complementarily without Hierarchy, (Downers Grove, IL: Intervarsity, 2005), 82.

[2] Ibid., 84.

[3] Richard S. Hess, "Discovering Biblical Equality: Complementarily Without Hierarchy," A Book Discussion. Chapter 4 – Equality With and Without Innocence: Genesis 1-3. *http:www kruse_kronicle/2006/10/discovering_bib_1.html* (15 January 2008).

[4] Valerie Sinason, "Abuse," The New Dictionary of Pastoral Studies, edited by Wesley Carr (Michigan: W.B. Eerdmans Publications, 2002), 2.

[5] Pamela Cooper, Turn Mourning into Dancing! A Policy Statement on Healing Domestic Violence (Louisville: The Office of the General Assembly, 2001), 15.

[6] United Nation General Assembly "85th plenary meeting20 December 1993". 48/104. Declaration on the Elimination of Violence against Women, Article 1 "The Violence Against Women". *http://www.un.org/documents/ga/res/48/a48r104. htm A/RES/48/104. (accessed 16 March 2016).*

Chapter 2

Socio - Cultural Perspectives
of the Abuse of Women

Spiritual, social, educational, traditional and cultural factors have a key role in influencing the upbringing of an individual and the family. These factors have great significance as it moulds the outlook towards women by society. A healthy society recognizes, and is familiar with, the role and potential of women and commits itself to promote all who contribute to improving conditions, status in society, and total well-being of women of all communities and ages. This chapter focuses on the impact of these socio-cultural characteristics on the abuse of women, with special reference to Christian families in India.

The Protection of Women from Domestic Violence Act (PWDVA) 2006 defines domestic violence, "that is comprehensive and includes all forms of physical, emotional, verbal, sexual, and economic violence, and covers both actual acts of such violence and threats of violence."[1]

Women, who are illiterate, less educated, belong to a low caste and tribe or low socio-economic groups are the worst affected victims, but abuse happens even in a highly educated, high income and upper class family.

According to Kounteya Sinha, even with the rise in education levels in India, in effect, "Over 40% of women in a nationwide survey are reported being beaten by their husbands at some point of time."[2] This beating can be serious, causing damage to health. It is quite amazing to note that, "Over 40% of married women experience abuse at home, only 2% of abused women have ever sought police help."[3] Probably they do not want publicity, bringing disgrace to self and family. The long-lasting and slow course of action of the judicial system perhaps forces them not to go for any legal help. The whole process needs finances, political influence and at times muscle power that may not be readily available for these harassed women. "Over four percent of women, fifty-one percent of men say it is all right for husband to beat his wife."[4] National Family Health Survey III has given some shocking news which says 1/10 women experienced sexual violence and 1/6 experienced emotional violence. According to Indian NFHS-III, "the worst violence was faced by women aged 25-29 years (24%)."[5] At the prime of their life, they face abuse. This statistic is very shocking. One-fourth of the women in India are denied their rights and privileges. Improvement is there; however in our society a large number of women still experience sexual discrimination.

ABUSE

Abuse is a broad subject as it is a universal issue and exists all over the world. Victim suffers due to gross injustices as a consequence of cultural, regional or religious practices. In abuse of women it is an ill- treatment by her close partners for reasons best known to them. Abuse is defined as, "the wilful infliction of physical injury, emotional anguish, or both on another person."[6]

Abuse has been normally explained as a form of bullying, whereby abusers exert power by violence because they fear they have no other means of control over the situation due to their irritating, egocentric and angry behaviour. Abusive behaviour keeps one partner in a position of power or control or domination over the other partner with fear, and intimidation. It may result in bruises, severe physical injuries, miscarriage (in the case of pregnant women) and mental agony. It can also cause long-term physical or psychological damage to the victim. According to Kounteya Sinha, "62% experienced physical or sexual abuse within the first two years of marriage while 32% experienced abuse in the first five years."[7] This may be due to the lack of knowledge about human sexuality and the bad influence of customs and traditions.

Women from the low socio-economic group may not have any domestic help. They attend to all the domestic chores like washing clothes, cooking, drawing water, cleaning the house, taking care of the elderly, children, and sick in the family. Due to this domestic situation, most of the time, she forgets her food and overlooks her own health. According to Indian culture, she is expected to do this as a submissive wife with no assistance from her husband. Even her medical needs are uncared for or neglected as no one cares to find out about her health. In the work area abuse continues. She is made to work with less wages when compared to her male colleagues doing the same job. They may not even be getting any benefits ensured by the Labour Law. She is also forced to put up with abuse at the work place because of her submissive nature.

"Abusers can be considered of two types, namely active and passive abusers. Active abusers are found in marital homes, and include in-laws or husband's relatives and friends. Passive abusers may be found in the neighbourhood or in the community; they act as if they are gentlemen but behave in opposite ways."[8]

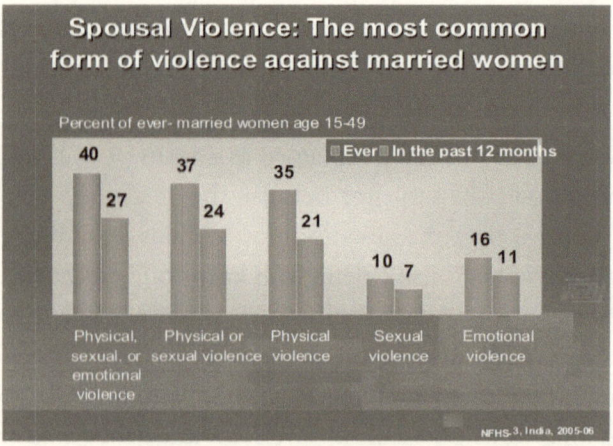

Abuse can take many forms and variations and can happen once in a while. The forms of abuse can be verbal, psychological, social, financial, physical, spiritual and sexual.

According to the National Family Health Survey -3, India during the year 2005-2006, the common forms of abuse experienced by the married women are given. It is self explanatory.

Gender Violence throughout the Life Cycle[9]

Phase	Type of violence present
Pre-birth	Sex-Selective abortion (China, India, Republic of Korea); battering during pregnancy (emotional and physical effects on the woman; effects on birth outcome); coerced pregnancy (for example, mass rape in war).
Infancy	Female infanticide; emotional and physical abuse; differential access to food and medical care for girl infants.
Girlhood	Child marriage; genital mutilation; sexual abuse by family members and strangers; differential access to food and medical care; child prostitution
Adolescence	Dating and courtship violence (for example, acid throwing in Bangladesh, date rape in the United States); economically coerced sex (African secondary school girls having to take up with "sugar daddies" to afford school fees); sexual abuse in the workplace; rape; sexual harassment; forced prostitution; trafficking in women.
Reproductive	Abuse of women by intimate male partners; marital rape; dowry abuse and age, murders; partner homicide; psychological abuse; sexual abuse in the workplace; sexual harassment; rape; abuse of women with disabilities
Elderly	Abuse of widows; elder abuse (in the United States, the only country where data are now available, elder abuse affects mostly of women).

Other forms of abuse against women include the practice of sex selective abortion and female infanticide. Sexual pestering or harassment at the work place; forced prostitution and trafficking are other forms of abuse. Some of the common types of abuse of woman are rape, wife battering and burning, dowry harassment by husband and in-laws especially during the time of pregnancy, exploitation, forced abortions, physical attacks, intimidation, restriction of normal activities and individual freedom, denial of access to resources and the ability to form close links with other women or the outside world, doubting the honesty and integrity of the person, and forced and obligatory prostitution.

Domestic abuse or violence is the term used to describe any abusive behaviour within an intimate relationship between two people. Normally, people will first think of physical violence, such as hitting, punching or slapping. But domestic abuse also covers emotional, verbal, sexual and financial behaviour perpetrated by one person on another within an intimate relationship. It affects adversely men and women, old and young, heterosexual couples and homosexual couples alike.

Following are some of the general characteristics of an abused individual. They have low levels of self-esteem, poor self concept; they are too emotional and are economically dependent, they feel depressed almost all the time and may be nervous or anxious. They feel socially isolated and may contemplate or attempt suicide or harm themselves; they often accept blame and guilt for abuse; they often suffer disorders through stress or psychosomatic complaints, consider leaving the relationship, behave like stereotypical sex roles; sometimes they accept the blame but at other times feel guilty; they have a wrong concept of the Christian faith and hope.

Research would also seem to indicate that victims of domestic abuse have a higher incidence of alcohol or drug abuse than non-victims. According to *Stark & Flitcraft (1996)*, "women who experience domestic abuse or violence are 15 times more likely to have alcohol dependency and 9 times more likely to have a drug problem than women not experiencing domestic violence."[10]

Domestic violence is a pattern of rude behaviours used by one individual intended to exercise authority, power and control over another individual in the context of an intimate relationship. It is a serious and an on-going problem that occurs in every culture and social group. It has different physical, emotional, financial and social effects on women, children, families, and communities around the world. Domestic Violence is defined as, "violence that occurs within a family system; is often used interchangeably with abuse; it includes physical abuse, neglect, psychological abuse, economic abuse, and sexual abuse."[11]

Abuse against women, is 'gender biased,' and jeopardizes women's lives as a whole, psychological integrity and freedom of choice. Abuse is likely to happen to people in a weaker position or to those who are agreeable to be accommodating or compromising for everything.

The Cycle of Abuse[12]

The cycle of abuse given below explains what happens before, during, and after an abuse. There are four phases for this process.

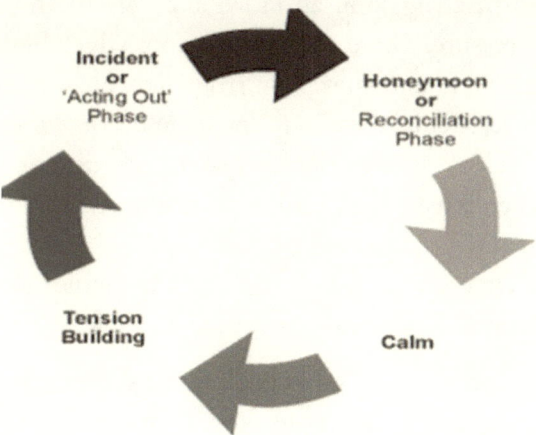

The above chart is a simplified one.

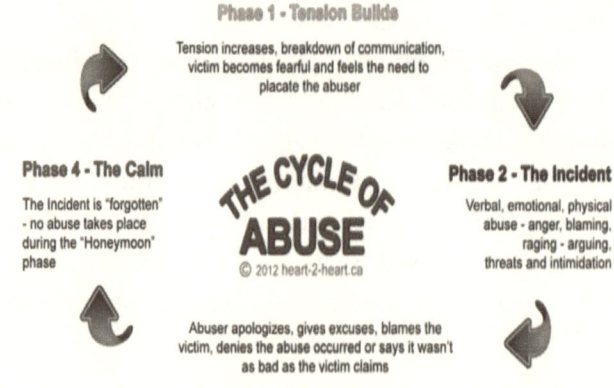

The first phase, the Tension Building Phase (TBP), starts with minor irritations from every side, finding fault with the spouse without any genuine reason, using bad language, making insults in front of friends, relative and family members, and restricting freedom in going out or meeting people. There is a gradual rise of tension during which the abuser uses emotional and verbal forms of abuse. Tension is a mental conflict or struggle in an individual's life often with signs of physiological pressure. There are many reasons which build up tension in an individual's life and they vary from individual to individual or culture to culture. Mental tension is due to an unforgiving spirit, anger, failures in life, lack of patience, ineffective communication and sickness. The uncontrolled tension can lead an individual to show evidence of abusive behaviour. When tension builds up, the abuser starts to get angry, and the victim feels uneasy and uncomfortable. The process of abuse is accelerated by a breakdown in communication.

The Actual Incident (AI) takes place in the second phase. Duration of this phase varies from hours to days. During this phase there is a possibility of the victim being sexually abused, physically injured or even killed. Although the abusive actions are the choice of the abuser, the victim is blamed for his actions.

The third phase, the Honeymoon Phase (HP), is also known as reconciliation phase or the calm and remorseful phase. Following the actual incident, the abuser may apologize, seek forgiveness from his partner, vouch never to repeat the abusive behaviour, show kindness and shower her with appreciative words and gifts. The abuser may assure his wife that he will never act aggressively again. The victim wants to believe this and may place her hope in his words and not seek help. This phase of the cycle may continue for a long period of time, but will eventually end as tension again begins to build. This is a vicious circle. This is followed by the reconciliation (honeymoon) phase where the abuser may feel guilty, asks for forgiveness or even say that he will not repeat it. There is calm in the next phase which does not last for long. There are various means for releasing tension. It is a traditional view or belief or unwritten law in India that men can get angry at any time for any reason and in the presence of anyone.

A husband who is not able to control his emotion of anger or tension repeats the cycle of abuse over and over again. It may be because of his personality traits and problem areas of his life which are intensified. In an effort to cover up his inadequacies he will abuse her more or become an alcoholic or substance abuser.

The cycle of abuse is rarely broken without outside help from clergy or professional counsellors, or psychiatrists. Both victim and abuser need to consider outside help to stop the cycle of abuse. Otherwise the abuser has to decide and determine to stop his inhuman action. No one understands the dynamics of cyclical abuse more than God. Divine intervention is indispensable. He has much to say about the nature of true repentance.

In 2 Corinthians 7:8-10, the apostle Paul mentions a Godly kind of sorrow; the kind that leads to turning away from wrong and inhuman behaviour. Genuine sorrow for abusive behaviour which results in true repentance is God's answer to the cycle of abuse. The Apostle Paul says that all fall short of the Glory of God.

Types of Abuses

Physical Abuse

Physical abuse can, and often does, cause serious physical harm, and often requires immediate medical attention or intervention. Abuse may start with a small shove during an argument, or forcefully grabbing one's wrist. Physical abuse usually becomes more severe, and more frequent, and can often result in severe bruises or even in the death of the victim.

Physical abuse is defined as "an act or conduct causing bodily pain, harm, or danger to life, limb, or health; an act that impairs the health or development of the aggrieved person; an act that amounts to assault, criminal intimidation, and criminal force."[13] Another definition for physical abuse is, "physical harm or injury caused by beating, hitting, cutting, shooting, burning, or raping; assault or threat of violence; battering is repeated physical abuse."[14]

Therefore physical abuse can be any form of causing injury, hitting, denying medical care or forced alcohol or drug use, slapping, beating, grabbing, kicking, shoving, choking, pinching, forced feeding, pulling hair, punching, throwing things, burning with cigarette or candle or lamp, strangling, use of weapons like guns, knives, or any other object, physical restraint - pinning against wall or floor or bed, and reckless driving. This is the most obvious, heart breaking and fatal form of domestic abuse.

Sexual Abuse

The television, radio, newspapers, magazines, and electronic media are crowded with incidents of abuse, especially sexual abuse. In the modern world media plays a key role in bringing the hidden facts of abuse to the light. Rapes by friends, relatives, strangers or even parents abusing their own children are some of the examples of the shocking news that grips today's world.

Children are not exempted from sexual abuse in India. Here is an unpleasant incident reported by *The Times of India* newspaper; the title was, *Kids forced to have oral sex at Haryana shelter*.[15] Children of five to ten years were forced into oral sex and performing yoga in the nude in a shelter home. In May 2012, this home was raided by National Commission for Protection of Child Rights (NCPCR). The children who were abused reported to the Commission that they were abused sexually. Church related institutions or NGO's in India are not an exemption.

Sexual abuse and sexual temptations are not new to us. Christians are not exceptions to this. News through the media reports of priests who have molested children and women, of nuns being raped or molested or an evangelist or clergy who has committed adultery. "Sexual abuse occurs when one person invades the physical or psychological space of another without consent or performs sexual acts on the victim. As a result of this invasion, the victims suffer physical or psychological harm or both."[16]

Sexual abuse can be defined, "as any sexual encounter without consent and includes any unwanted touching, forced sexual activity, forcing the victim to perform sexual acts, painful or degrading acts during or after intercourse, and exploitation through pornography or prostitution'. Sexual abuse or a threat of sexual abuse includes, 'any conduct of a sexual nature that abuses, humiliates, degrades, or otherwise violates the dignity of a woman."[17] Sex on demand or sexual withholding, physical assaults or non-consensual sex, denying or forced sexual intercourse, forced sexual contact, inappropriate touching or control of reproductive freedom are also considered as sexual abuse. Sexual jokes that make the victim uncomfortable, treating women as sex objects, criticizing the victim's sexuality, forcing the victim to watch or to witness or participate in sexual activity with others, and sexual torture. The Madurai High court in Tamilnadu passed a verdict that, "wilful denial of sexual intercourse either on the part of a husband or wife will come under the contours of mental cruelty as per Section 13(1) (ia) of the Hindu marriage act."[18]

Sudhir Kakkar has estimated that, "at least 600,000 to 700,000 Indian children are likely to have experienced sexual abuse, mostly by members of their own families."[19]

Cultural Abuse

Culture is the sum total of the values, attitudes, beliefs, gender relations, practices of child rearing, and prevailing norms. It is the economic, political, social and spiritual organization of people's way of life. Some cultures have evolved from living in a context over a period of several years, some through migration, trade, colonization, and lately globalization. Cultural motives or systems can cause abuse, e.g., female feticide and female infanticide, conscious neglect of the health and education of girl children and female genital mutilation or ill-treating the girl child. The boy child is precious; during pregnancy extra care is given to mother so that she will deliver a healthy boy child.

As a result of colonization and Christianity being spread to different parts of the world, there was a vast improvement in the field of education, health, job, family, life style and value system. The status of women started to improve slowly and steadily.

Structural Abuse

Family, community and religious institutions offer a sense of identity and belonging. They themselves could become instruments of abuse. Despite this, women are expected to be the guardians of, and play roles in these very same structures. Men also feel restricted or constrained by the roles they are expected to play. Structural abuse often goes unnoticed or overlooked and is collectively maintained and validated in the name of order and stability.

Victims can be individuals, groups, or a collective body. The law enforcers may change but the structures remain the same. Men are given societal power over women in Indian culture; but when this power is used in an unhealthy and harmful way to control and oppress, it becomes an abuse. Many women believe that they are powerless; they are taught and often made to believe that abuse is deserved. In addition, many societies do little to stop or reduce abuse, e.g., even where explicit laws against domestic abuse exist. Police, courts, and even clergyman often neglect or do not take this problem of abuse very seriously and with urgency.

Emotional / Psychological Abuse

Emotional abuse hurts or creates deep wounds which leaves scars on the mind of a person and has a lifelong impact. Physical or sexual abuse is always accompanied by emotional abuse. Ignoring or discounting activities and accomplishments; withholding approval or affection; embarrassing, and humiliating in public or in front of children and other family members or friends, being irrational and suspicious, creating fear by intimidation; threatening physical harm to self, spouse, or children; destruction of pets and property, mind games or forcing isolation from friends, family, and work; destructive criticism, pressure tactics and strategy; lying determinedly, not listening or responding to the wife's requests or talk; and monitoring phone calls, emails, and letters, making nasty jokes about the victim, insulting, ignoring the victim's feelings, yelling at the victim, blaming the victim for everything, and threatening to take children away from the victim are a few examples of emotional abuse.

It is often difficult to identify psychological abuse. Although psychological abuse does not leave any noticeable bruises physically, it leaves many imperceptible scars physiologically on the self-esteem or the self-image of the individual. This is more destructive and damaging to the individual than any other factor.

Self-esteem is the degree to which we view self- worth as a person. The foundation of our self-image is first formed in childhood and continues in life until the last breath we take. Low self-esteem arises when an individual feels he is not as competent or as smart as others. The person who develops low or poor self-image from childhood may develop an inferiority complex. It is very difficult to change all of a sudden. This complex can lead to abuse. Also a person with low esteem cannot tolerate the other, and thus tries to manipulate any form of abuse to balance his low esteem. He may develop a character of unworthiness or shame; which can lead to loneliness, depression and poor self-concept. This is triggering factor of abuse.

Often the spouse exploits his mate's love and sympathy by being angry under the disguise of 'openness' and uses this to achieve his own goals. This manipulative or controlling process could severely and negatively harm marital relationships. Anger is manifested when we yield to extreme pressures from people or circumstances and say or do something that offends others. Anger is a human emotional response which can drive an individual to a healthy or unhealthy behaviour or attitude. It may range from minor impatience, irritation and then to intense rage. When anger gets out of control it becomes a destructive force rather than being constructive; it creates problems, tension, unrest, or unpleasantness in Indian Christian families, work areas and relationships. Unexpressed or constrained or hidden anger can create different types of physical, emotional and mental problems. Research has found that family background, childhood experiences and family atmosphere play a key role; other factors are physiological, cultural, and psychological.

All sorts of irritation or frustration can prompt anger. Envy or resentment is a strong negative emotion that can lead to anger. Anger that is a by product of unforgiveness usually festers on the inside of a person. Charles Spiel Berger Ph.D, a psychologist who specialized in the subject of anger, defines anger as "an emotional state that varies in intensity from mild irritation to intense fury and rage."[20] Like any another emotion, it is accompanied by physiological and biological changes in our body. Most of the time heart rate and blood pressure go up and also levels of adrenaline.

According to Dr. Laila Ahmed, "The three main approaches to healthy expression of anger are expressing, suppressing, and calming. Expressing your angry feelings in an assertive-not aggressive-manner is the healthiest way to express anger; to do this, you have to learn how to make clear what your needs are, and how to get them met, without hurting others. Being assertive doesn't mean being pushy or demanding; it means being respectful of yourself and others."[21] Anger suppressed inside can affect all the systems in the body. Anger suppressed, then transformed and turned inward may cause hypertension, depression or aggressive behaviour which affects the health.

Financial Abuse

Financial or economic abuse is defined as, "financial exploitation of a victim by restricting access to money, food, clothing or transportation."[22] Financial abuse includes keeping financial details away from the spouse, refusing or preventing to let the woman work even though she is capable of it, controlling the woman's access to cash, insisting on joint bank accounts, cheque books, credit cards, taking all the money from the victim' salary, refusing to pay any bills, forcing the victim to pay even though they both work, withholding all the funds available, spending family income without the consent of the spouse, and making the partner struggle to pay bills. The above are some of the examples of financial abuse. Financial blackmail occurs when women who have no income, are forced to become financially dependent on their husbands, often having to ask for money and abuse her for over spending. Money becomes an instrument used by the abuser to have power or control over the victim, ensuring her financial enslavement and dependence on him.

Quite often the husband is unable to meet financial obligations at home. The wife may be qualified to take up a job so that she will be partially independent financially or reduce the financial struggle at home. But the husband, with his inferiority complex or with the thoughts of male supremacy, does not permit her to seek employment. Some believe if she starts to work, then he has no control over her. She will also be more independent than ever, which he does not want. This will bring friction at home.

In recent times women have become financially more independent than in earlier days, due to the better jobs through their education and qualifications. They get better salaries and perks from their places of work. But some of these women never disclose to their spouse how much monthly salary and other perks they get. They have individual bank accounts without the knowledge of their spouse. If the husband enquires about it, they hide it or only tell half truths with lame excuses to protect their course of action. The wife does it with the reason that the husband does not wisely allocate the money, or misuse the money for unwanted things. This can be bad investments or mismanagement of finances, gambling, no control over funds and extravagances, spending money on parents, relatives or close friends, instead of considering family priorities. If the wife tries to control to any such kind of spending then he abuses his wife as being the cause of all financial turmoil in the family. But financial abuse happens due to lack of transparency in dealing with financial matters.

The Times of India has reported that a woman was set on fire by her husband, "Nagaraju doused Rangamma with kerosene and set her on fire following a quarrel after he pawned her jewellery in Soladevanahalli on July 29, 2007."[23] This incident also demonstrates the fact that husbands use their wives' jewellery as they like without a word to them before giving it to the pawn broker. Because she questioned her husband, she was set on fire.

Verbal Abuse

Verbal abuse can be defined, "as words that attack or injure an individual, words that cause one to believe an untrue statement, or words that speak falsely of an individual."[24]

One of the main focuses of the verbal abuse is to make a person feel *worthless*. Verbal abuse takes a tremendous emotional toll ! Here is a partial list of behaviour that is included in verbal abuse, "yelling, accusing, using sarcasm, threatening, insulting, treating with scorn, intimidating, humiliating, putting down, ridiculing, blaming, disparaging ideas, name-calling, belittling, rejecting opinion, criticizing, mocking, trivializing desires."[25]

Verbal abuse does not have any bruises compared to physical battering. The victims of verbal abuse live in a confusing and unrealistic world.

Spiritual Abuse

Persecution, discrimination or ill treatment from secular authorities is not spiritual abuse. But any discrimination and harassment from religious authorities or husband and senior members in the family is considered as spiritual abuse. This leaves the person spiritually discouraged, disappointed and emotionally cut off from the love of God.

Spiritual abuse can normally occur when a leader uses his or her spiritual position to control or dominate another individual. It often involves intervening the feelings and opinions of another, without regard to what will result in the other person's state of living, emotions or well-being. It can also occur when spirituality is used to make others live up to a spiritual maturity. Spiritual abuse is, "the mistreatment of an individual who is in need of help, support or greater spiritual empowerment, with the result of weakening, undermining or decreasing that person's spiritual empowerment."[26]

Ronald Enroth defines Spiritual abuse as, "when leaders to whom people look for guidance and spiritual nurture use their positions of authority to manipulate, control, and dominate."[27] "Spiritual abuse occurs when someone in a position of spiritual authority, the purpose of which is to 'come underneath' and serve, build, equip and make God's people more free, misuses that authority placing themselves over God's people to control, coerce or manipulate them for seemingly godly purposes which are really their own."[28]

Spiritual abuse is not limited to any particular religion or denomination. Any person is capable of perpetrating spiritual abuse, just as anyone can be the victim of it. It leaves a great impact on any individual, especially woman's self-esteem and confidence; make a woman feel guilty, damage her spiritual experiences and isolate her. Spiritual abuse is misusing God's name, by misinterpreting God's plan for their wrong doing. Whenever anyone is dehumanized in the name of God, it is spiritual abuse. Spiritual abuse is crafty, manipulating to keep one's power. When someone in a position of marriage or family authority misuses that authority by placing themselves over God's plan for healthy parenting and leadership, their desire is to control, coerce or manipulate family for seemingly personal reasons.

Spiritual abuse has a very prominent place in the Bible, though that terminology has not been used until recently. In the scripture it is called bondage to men and the traditions of men. It is a by-product and outgrowth of legalism, which is bondage to the letter of the law.

This cause hurt in manner and damages the personality of others by acting in an authoritarian and self-centered manner in order to benefit themselves. The husbands often quote Biblical passages about giving generously to God and his hidden agenda is to control her spending. At times to control her social life, he speaks about faithfulness in marriage. Ridiculing 'single women' 'women living alone', 'widows' during the sermon is nothing but spiritual abuse. In many denominations, men and women are not permitted to marry outside their denomination. If such marriage takes place they are considered as 'second class citizens' or ex-communicated from the church.

Following are the few ways of a abusive spiritual individual ridiculing or insulting the another individual's religious or spiritual concepts, principle and beliefs, preventing from practicing their routine religious or spiritual beliefs /rituals, forcing the children to be raised in a faith that the other partner has not agreed to, and accusing a individual of being too religious or not religious enough, not allowing to practice any religion,read spiritual books, listen to sermon or spiritual discourse, attending spiritual meeting, entertaining spiritual leaders.

It is also common in many parts of our country that women are forced to stay at the *House of Prayer* (prayer hall) for fasting and praying if she is childless, having some illness, for improving family finances, for moulding the children's character, for deliverance from evil spirit etc. Many times she will be drugged, sexually abused, at times physically beaten to chase away the evil spirit in this place. These scars can never heal.

Many men indulge in practicing sorcery, witchcraft or black magic with the pretext of improving finances, getting a male child, or to bring harm on others. Many times we read in the newspaper that children are sacrificed by the father, marriages are conducted for animals - everything done with advice of God -man for improving agriculture, for rains in drought areas etc. Here again the women is forced to follow all rituals and later to be part of the pooja (worship). Women with strong Christian belief are forced to engage into these wrong deeds. She cannot refuse or inform anyone as she may lose other children or she will be branded as someone with bad character.

Social Abuse

Social abuse is a form of segregation or separation or isolation; the abuser may try to hold back or doesn't allow any type of social interaction or communication of the victim with friends or relatives. The family demands the woman to be at home all the time so that she has no time or opportunity for socializing with her loved ones or friends. The abuser also ensures that necessary facilities are not provided especially conveyance, telephone, finance, or escort; if she goes out he demands a report on actions and conversations or harsh questioning immediately on arrival. Suspicion makes the abuser closely check all the activities of his wife or at times he instructs the children or friends to watch her moments. Close circuit cameras are fixed in all the rooms to observe her closely. The other causes are substance abuse, alcoholism, gambling, influence of cult teachings, changing trends of the family concept, harassment in working areas, inter-caste and inter–religious marriage, and vast age difference between the couple.

Abuse of women has a social impact on human society and in the Christian community as a whole. The impact includes medical and legal costs along with services that have to be set up to treat victims of violence as well as for services that have to be set up to prevent gender based violence. Social costs include the neglect of children and the negative impact on their health, nutrition, education and on their individual growth. It also perpetuates inter generational violence. Stresses and strains of life are often borne by women who are victims of violence. Women have sought alternative survival strategies in contractual overseas employment, only to be confronted with violence as workers confined to the domestic sphere away from public scrutiny while their children are subjected to neglect and abuse as well. Abuse of women not only affects the spouses, but also their children, parents, relatives and the community they are living in. One of the main reasons for abuse of women in Christian families is the misuse of power and control, cultural influences, unnecessary interference by in-laws, friends and wrong teachings leaving more room for abuse.

In today's world, our safety and privacy could be compromised via physical, social or emotional abuse or electronically via crude SMS, hacked accounts, hacked systems, personal data & pictures being accessed from computers and phones. This could happen in our personal space in work area or in the public transport system. Prying perverts, snooping husbands, relatives, friends share personal details in social media. Printing, releasing or conveying obscene acts, photos in public is on the rise. The causes for social abuse of women are numerous. As it is not possible to narrate all the causes, the author will narrow it down to dowry, lack of support in nuclear family, illegal sex determination tests leading to abortion, and the patriarchal system.

Dowry

Dowry is defined as "the payment in cash or property of any kind by the bride's family to the bridegroom's family along with the giving away of the bride, known as Kanyadaan in Indian marriage."[29] Kanyadaan or 'stridhan' is an important part of Hindu marital rites. Kanya means 'daughter', and Dana means 'gift'. Since 2005, many parents feel that marriage is no more 'Kanyadaan', known as gift of a daughter but 'Putr Samarpan'(handing over of son to the daughter-in-law. [30] It is a bride price.

Dowry originated 'in upper caste families voluntarily and not by any external force as a wedding gift to the bride by her family. [31] Dowry was later considered as a help rendered for the marriage expenses. It was also meant to be used for future needs if she was ill-treated by the in-laws or became a widow. Dowry was legally prohibited in India since 1961. The original purpose of the dowry was overtaken by greed on the part of the groom or his parents. Now the term 'dowry' is not publically used but giving in cash or kind to the groom's family is still in practice. Unfortunately it has become a commercial transaction in which monetary considerations receive priority over the personal merits of the bride and have turned the sanctity of relationship in the marriage into a commercial relationship.

Dowry is a social menace and is one of the main reasons for abuse of married women. In arranged marriages, the groom and bride decide to leave the decision of their impending marriage to their parents and relatives. The groom's parents makes an announcement that they are not demanding dowry but they will accept gifts (it may vary from acres of land, fully furnished house, expensive vehicle, electronic items, household items, jewellery, pocket money so on and so forth) that the girl's family have to willingly give. The bride's parents have to oblige hence they promise all gifts to groom. Extravagant wedding ceremony has become the norm. Marriages are now looked upon as an opportunity to improve family status through huge amounts of money, gold and other perks which in turn lead to a new social standing.

At times even at the wedding ceremony or wedding receptions or afterwards, humiliating remarks are made about the ornaments or wedding arrangements to the bride or their family. This continues when the bride is taken to the in- law's house. It is a common practice in rural areas to invite neighbours and display the ornaments and exhibit the articles brought by the bride. Later these ornaments are checked for its purity, fashion and quantity by experts. The neighbours may make belittling comments on the bride probably for out fashioned ornaments and for bringing less number of household articles or compare her to other brides in that area who brought much more and are supposed to be beautiful. This may lead to physical abuse if the bride resists. She will be forced to contact her parents for more money or articles. Later she is sent back to her home with a stipulation that she can come back only if she meets the demand of her husband's family.

A few husbands may not send them immediately but will constantly abuse and harass her, thus making her life miserable and creating an urge to force her family to give more and more. In order to sustain the marriage, the wife decides to tolerate the abuse to avoid further embarrassment. The lack of receptiveness from the wife's family results in the abuse becoming more severe and it intensifies day by day. Later on the husband and his family decide on plans for another alliance where they can demand more, in this process wife and her family are humiliated or forced to yield their demands. Getting rid of the wife becomes a necessity for some due to the greed for money. They will look for the opportunities and will attempt to brutally kill her or constantly ill-treat her. Murder may be interpreted as suicide and the cases remain unsolved. The researcher has personally known few families where the husband marries a second time for monetary benefit and the first wife then has a lower status when compared to the second wife.

Dowry Deaths

Dowry deaths are deaths of women who are murdered privately or driven to suicide by constant abuse and torture by husbands and in-laws in an effort to extract dowry or an increased dowry.

Recent data reveals very shocking news that twenty two dowry deaths are reported across the country daily. There are unusual difficulties in ascertaining the nature of death particularly when good amount of planning has gone into the preparation of crime and when perpetrators have sufficient opportunity to destroy the evidences. For analyzing in proper manner, death cases can be broadly grouped as dowry death due to burns, drowning, hanging, strangulation, throttling and poisoning.

With constant harassment, the wife not finding any way out may decide to end her life. Many mothers kill their girl child along with them also so that this child need not face harassment in future. Through this untimely death, we are losing many talented, young, energetic, gifted women and promising generation who could have contributed much for the family, community, women folks, society or the country at large. This will cause a decline in ratio of men: women.

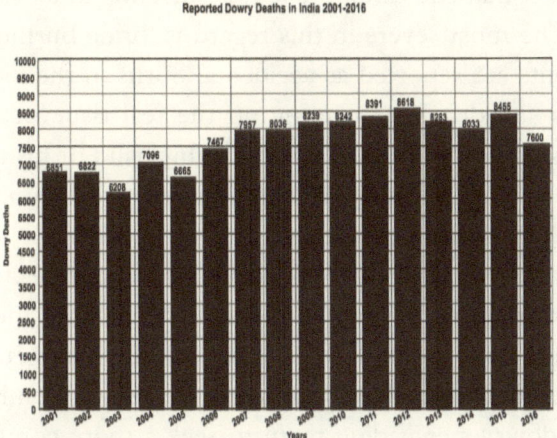

The graph above portray dowry death in India from the year 2001 to 2016.[32]

At what Periods of Marital Duration does Spousal Violence first Occur?[33]

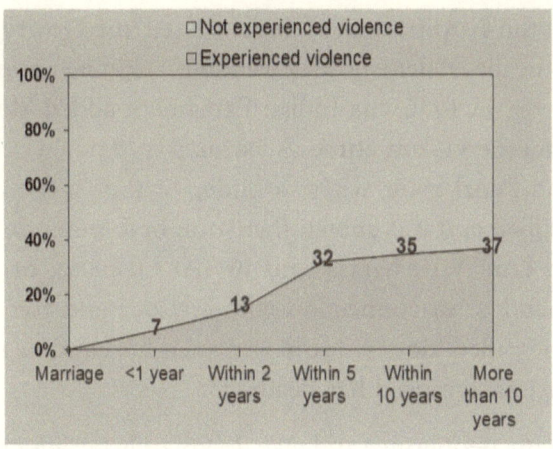

NHFS- 3, India, 2005-2006

In broad-spectrum, the woman decides to accept the abuse silently because social customs and traditions enforce silence of the abuse. Not only verbal abuse, serious physical and psychological abuse also takes place which may even result in the death or suicide of women due to the fact that she cannot take this suffering in its various forms any more. The most severe in this regard is 'bride burning'. Most of these incidents are reported as accidental burns in the kitchen or are disguised as suicide, thus covering up the real issue of abuse. This abuse can escalate to the point where the husband or his family burns the bride, often by pouring kerosene on her and lighting it, usually killing her. The official records of these incidents are low because the family often reports them as accidents or suicides. Many times the senior women in the family demand dowry and media reports that women were also involved in harassing the younger women for dowry. Older men in the family influence the young men in the family to demand dowry, persuading them to seek a more comfortable life, financial security and improved social status. Unfortunately a few men fall prey to this.

Despite the existence of rigorous laws to prevent dowry-deaths under the 1986 amendment to the Indian Penal Code (IPC), convictions are rare.

In 1961, the Government of India passed 'the Dowry Prohibition Act' to stop the illegal demands for wedding, wedding arrangements, or plans. However, in 1986, the Indian Parliament added 'dowry deaths' as a new domestic violent crime. According to the new section 304-B of the Indian Penal code, where a bride, "within seven years of her marriage is killed and it is shown that soon before her death, she was subjected to cruelty or harassment by her husband, or any relative of her husband or in connection with any demand for dowry, such death shall be called 'dowry death' and such husband or relative shall be deemed to have caused her death."[34]

Today many people give and take dowry only because their parents and ancestors practiced it. Many girls remain unmarried as their parents cannot afford or fulfil the demand of the boy's parents to pay a large amount of money as dowry.

Illegal Sex Determination

Women are every now and then seen as an apparatus for child bearing. Most of the time, the husband and his family want only a boy child. Even in early pregnancy, the wife may be forced to go for sex determination. Often it is against her wishes. The psychological trauma she undergoes is immeasurable and disregards her womanhood.

There is a great celebration when a boy child is born. Families start planning his future while the child is still a baby. At the same time, we hear about girl babies abandoned in the hospitals and dead female foetuses found in dustbins. There is a steady increase in illegal medical practitioners who encourage illegal sex determination and abortion for monetary benefits.

35

Sex Ratio (Females/1000 Males)

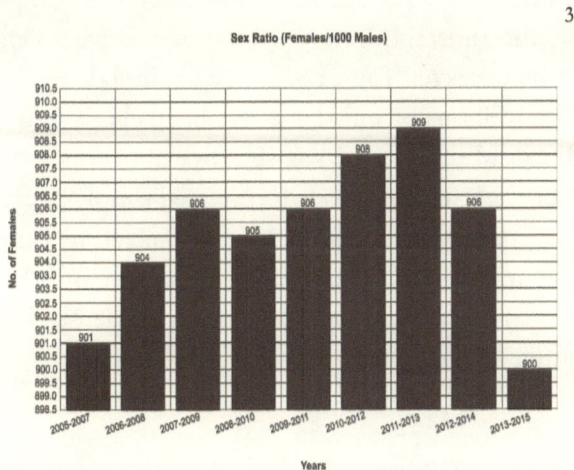

"The sharp decline in the sex ratio is a matter of serious concern as it is expected to lead to serious demographic imbalances in the future. One of the causes may be due to illegal abortion of the female foetus. There is no doubt that this practice, if continued, will shackle the very social fabric of our nation."[36] The reason for unequal access to life of girls in India has roots in economic, religious, sexual, and cultural dynamics. There are many cultural and socio-economic reasons that can be attributed to this practice. Diagnostic teams with ultra sound scanners, which detect the sex of a child, advertise, "Spend 600 rupees now and save 50,000 rupees later. By avoiding a girl, a family will avoid paying a large dowry on the marriage of daughter.'[87]

"Millions of women have gone missing from our India's population due to deep-seated male favoritism and excessive son inclination. According to a recent report from the Government of India, a staggering 63 million women are now missing from India's population. The report further estimates that an additional 21 million girls are unwanted by their parents who would have preferred a boy instead. The figures were released by the Indian Ministry of Finance in its Economic Survey 2017-2018. There are a number of reasons why the gender gap between men and women in India is so large. For one, many women in India suffer significantly diminished access to healthcare, adequate nutrition, education, and other resources compared to men. As a result, the mortality rate for women relative to men is higher than would be expected for a country with India's level of economic development. Millions of girls have also been eliminated prior to birth by the widespread practice of sex-selective abortion, a discriminatory practice where girls are selectively terminated simply because they were not boys. Even after birth, girls may be subjected to various kinds of neglect, receiving less food, healthcare, education, or other necessities. This appears to be particularly true if they happen to be a second or third daughter.'[88]

Abortion

Abortion is defined, "as termination of pregnancy before the foetus becomes viable."[39] Some of the abortion cases take place without the mutual consent of both partners.

The Medical Termination of Pregnancy (MTP) Act, 1971. Section 3, says that pregnancy can be terminated only under certain conditions. The MTP bill was passed by both Houses of Parliament and received the assent of the President of India on April, 1972. The MTP law guarantees the Right of Women in India to terminate an unintended pregnancy by a registered medical practitioner in a hospital established or maintained by the Government or a place approved for the purpose of this Act by the Government. Not all pregnancies could be terminated. The conditions under which a pregnancy can be terminated under MTP Act 1971 are as follows:

> A medical condition, where continuation of the pregnancy might endanger the mother's life or cause grave injury to her physical or mental health; Eugenic, where there is substantial risk of the child being born with serious handicaps due to physical or mental abnormalities; Humanitarian, where pregnancy is the result of rape; Socio-economic, where actual or reasonably foreseeable environment (whether social or economic) could lead to risk of injury to the health of the mother; failure of contraceptive devices. The anguish caused by an unwanted pregnancy resulting from a failure of any contraceptive device or method can be presumed to constitute a grave mental injury to the health of the mother. This condition is a unique feature of the Indian law and virtually allows abortion on request in view of the difficulty of proving that a pregnancy was not caused by failure of contraception.[40]

Abortion can be considered as murder. Abortion of the girl child is most common. So this becomes the cruel form of abuse against women. The foetal heart develops and begins to beat as early as four weeks after conception. The mother feels the foetal movements between 16 to 20 weeks of pregnancy. The continued existence may be expected if the baby is born from 24-28 weeks with adequate medical care. Killing the foetus is a sin and is condemned by Christianity. Aborting a foetus is a cruelty causing physical and psychological abuse to the unborn child. In almost all cases illegal sex determination is meant for the abortion of the female foetus.

Even with these existing laws, abortions are conducted by qualified medical practitioners as well as quacks for monetary benefits. The medical indications for abortion are entered wrongly in the medical report. The mother is psychologically tormented lifelong with the thoughts of losing a child as it was against her will. Causing miscarriage without the consent of the women is common. Certain herbs are forcibly given to the pregnant lady to cause abortion. Sharp object or weapon is inserted vaginally causing abortion and later lady dies of severe bleeding as medical attention was not given. It is sad to say that MTP in Christian hospitals are common and Christian doctors doing MTP in their clinics which are not be in accordance to the MTP Act because the request is made by the rich and influential people.

Inequalities in Society

In India, female discrimination and abuse is still a major issue. Women's rights can be violated when they are discriminated against their race, religious beliefs or socio-economic conditions and their sex.

Pandit Jawarlal Nehru, the first Prime Minister of India, on the eve of India's independence wrote, "The spirit of the age is in favour of equality, though practice denies it almost everywhere."[41] Through this, he is calling for change in society. Tagore and Gandhi both expressed the same view.

Each individual is assured of equality of status and opportunity for the development of the best and the means for the enforcement of the rights are guaranteed to each individual according to the Indian Penal Code. Discrimination between citizen and citizen, simply on the ground of religion, race, caste, sex or place of birth, is illegal (Article 15).

Inequality exists in employing women in various posts, while wages for the same jobs are paid differently for men and women. In India if we look into the number of Parliament seats occupied by women, they are fewer when compared with men. Equality in opportunity and ability is mostly denied to women. When women react to these inequalities, they are liable to be abused rather than understood. Certain cultural and religious practices can have an enormous impact on a woman's rights. The political climate of a country or region can affect the state of women rights. Women throughout the ages have suffered oppression. For example, women in certain areas of the world have not had access to good education which denies them the chance to seek proper employment and build an independent future.

Hierarchy in Family Roles

The hierarchy in family roles can also become a factor for abuse of married women. Male dominance forces women to be suppressed, oppressed and ill-treated. She wants to resist but it is impossible. She is threatened by male supremacy and muscle power. This reaction can be a reason for the husband to start abuse causing psychological, verbal, physical abuse in women.

Age and sex are two main factors in family hierarchy. According to M.S. Gore, "Men have the more decisive authority in the traditional Indian family as compared with women and elders have greater authority compared with young persons."[42] The man is always considered to be superior due to his masculinity and has been seen as the decision maker according to the patriarchal system. This system follows male dominance and the concept of women playing second fiddle. The males try to prove their masculinity or to make the rules because they are afraid of being categorized as hen- pecked. This statement can be explained with a simple example: in certain communities, the female flocks are not supposed to eat at the dining table along men and are expected to serve the food. They are allowed to eat in the kitchen once the men complete eating and wife is expected to eat in the plate in which her husband ate. These examples may appear not worth mentioning, but are attached to the concept of serving the strong.

Patriarchy (Greek ' *patria* ' meaning 'father' and ' *arche* ' meaning 'rule') is an anthropological term used to define, "the sociological condition where male members of a society tend to predominate in positions of power; with the more powerful the position, the more likely it is that a male will hold that position. '[43] The dominant male limits her role and freedom in decision making in the family. In every patriarchal pattern there is a hierarchical structure. This structure exists in the Christian community and it subjugates women in the Church as well.

Throughout Indian history, women have had bad experiences and never-ending struggles to break away from the traditions of the patriarchal system. This male-dominant family structure expects women, "to live selflessly while properly carrying out all domestic duties."[44] Fortunately, social reformers during the early 19th century began to challenge the traditional roles of Indian women.

Religious Aspects

There are various religious factors which may lead to abuse of women as a result of ignorance or misapprehension. Those factors are narrated below.

Inter-religious Marriage

The Bible teaches us saying, "Do not be yoked together with unbelievers. For what do righteousness and wickedness have in common." (2 Cor. 6:14). In an inter-religious marriage, one partner may sacrifice attending ceremonial functions of their religion. His or her parents may not accept the spouse. Tension mounts up when decision on the religious beliefs on which the children to be brought up arises. When the child grows to be of marriageable age, choosing a partner from which religion is a matter of concern. All these may lead to strained inter-personal relationships, misunderstandings, maladjustment and, in turn, to abuse.

Misinterpretation of the Scripture

The Bible is often misinterpreted by some people according to their whims and fancies, which cause religious tension or conflict within the family. The concept of 'Submission' is misinterpreted if it is applicable only to the wife. She is expected to be quiet and to play an inferior role. The submission in the biblical view is mutual submission. Mutual submission means, 'to respect, honour, love and care for each other.' Biblical submission is always bonded with agape love. A woman who is well educated and talented is always told to be submissive; she finds it very difficult to adjust. Tension gradually builds up. If the husband is not able to understand her, he comes to the conclusion that she is disobedient and abuse becomes a regular feature in their family.

Excuses for Abuse

Husbands make excuses to justify themselves against criticism or opposition. Alcohol consumption is often used as an excuse for the abuse. Not all who take alcohol are abusers. They use alcohol as defence mechanism or as escapism from tensions and pressures in their lives.

Alcohol consumption is used to take revenge to their partner or to forget the problems in their lives.

The excuses of the husband go on to state that his wife's behaviour is not according to his expectation or anticipation, does not come up to his standards when compared to other women. Many a time his inner conflicts are displaced and projected as the fault of his wife. He feels that his wife is disobedient and arrogant when she is successful in her career. Sometimes his friends and his family encourage him to intimidate the wife because of her success. He thinks that the only way to suppress the success of his wife is to abuse her verbally, physically, mentally, and emotionally. He thinks that the choice of his marriage partner was wrong. Lack of freedom and too much restriction imposed on her, being accused for no fault of hers, and then being abused by the husband brings devastation in the family. The children view their father as rude and a cruel man. A father who continually abuses their mother does not match the children's expectations. There is lack of family bonding, split relationships and mistrust.

The wife suffers because of the autocratic, domineering and stubborn behavior and attitude of the husband. She may lack emotional support in time of agony or crisis. When a capable wife either shoulders or shares the family responsibilities, an egoistic husband may feel insulted or that he is being dominated.

The case studies illustrated below depict an assortment of abuse of women. In all these cases it started with verbal abuse, which then led to physical, psychological, financial, spiritual, social, and structure abuse, however, the cause of abuse differs.

Case Study 1

Mr. J[45] is a civil contractor in Bangalore who hails from the state of Kerala. He married Ms. S. His contract business was flourishing. Once, during the construction work, one of his workers fell down from the top of the building and died. He had to pay a huge compensation to settle the matter. This was an unforeseen and sudden event in his life. Most of his investments were gone within a day. His first-born was a girl child. After one-year a second girl child and two years later third girl child were born. The fourth child was also a girl. After the birth of all the girl children, he started to punch, beat, choke, kick, assault his wife with weapons, slap, and throw sharp objects at his wife's face, abusing her and continued torturing her and the children mentally. Consistently he abused her saying she gave birth only to girl children. He had expected only boys, so that in the future he could get dowry. Why couldn't she have delivered four boys instead of girls? He never gave her peace of mind. What did this poor lady do? Three of their daughters got married; yet he continues beating his wife.

His business failure, financial problems and lack of a male heir gave him an excuse to abuse. He assumed that it was all right to abuse her, as neither society nor his wife objected to it. The church never interfered in these matters.

He blames his wife, family, God and others for his misfortunes. Mrs. S believes that as a Christian and dutiful wife, she should silently bear all these sufferings as her reward in heaven will be great. Though many showed sympathy none came forward to help her.

Case Study 2

Here is a case story of a young couple named Mr. A[46] and Mrs. M. With great expectations, the marriage was arranged. Mr. A was working in UAE when he married Mrs. M. After his holidays were over, he went back to his working place leaving his wife in India. Four months later, he lost his job and returned to India. He started a business in his hometown along with some of his friends. All his savings, including his wife's dowry and ornaments, were invested in his business. Somehow, the business did not pickup as expected. All the money invested was lost. All his friends left him. Mr. A's family started blaming Mrs. M for all the misfortune. Mrs. M was abused verbally, physically, emotionally and socially.

Mrs. M suffered in silence, as she did not want a bad reputation for her family. His financial tension made him a substance abuser. He and his family strongly believed that all this had happened because of Mrs. M as everything started after the marriage. Mr. A's parents blamed her for being the root cause of failures in his business and life.

Case Study 3

Mr. R.[47] comes from a non-Christian background. He came to know the Lord during a convention. After basic training in theology, he was posted as an evangelist. He was a good preacher and soon became very famous. He married Ms. S who was from a middle class Christian family. They had three children, two girls, and one boy. Though he was considered to be very religious, righteous and an able preacher, it was a different picture while he was at home. He started fighting with his wife. He mercilessly beat his wife and children for simple reasons. His way of life and work necessitated meeting people at various places and having association with rich and educated people. Due to this association, it made him feel that his family was not up to the mark when compared to others. He often told his wife that he deserved a better family and that he had made a wrong choice also.

Here we can find that even those who are in active in ministry can also turn out to be abusers. He was able to hide the abuse while ministering to people. His family, particularly his children, wonder why he is not able to practice what he preaches or teaches in his family. There is no peace in the home.

Case Study 4

Recently a friend of mine narrated about a family. Mr. K[48], an under graduate hailing from a poor family fell in love with Ms. W who is rich, well educated, having a good job and parents are well settled. Finally they were married. After the marriage K told W that the entire monthly income should come to his account and the property which belong to her to be transferred to his name .She was not willing to yield to K's demands. After few months, argument, fight and physical harassment started. W returned to her parents. K spread gossip among her colleagues that she was having extra-marital relationship. She wanted divorce, but he decided not to divorce her but to harass emotionally.

From the above case studies we observe that husbands abuse their wives for different reasons. Further, we can get a glimpse of factors leading to abuse due to the socio-cultural aspects in Indian families.

Endnotes

[1] National Family Health Survey "(NFHS-4) Domestic Violence," 2017, 561.

[2] Kounteya Sinha, "54% women say wife-beating okay," *Times of India* (Bangalore), 12 October 2007, 1.

[3] Ibid.,1.

[4] Ibid.,1.

[5] Kounteya Sinha, "Slapping is most common abuse," *The Times of India* (Bangalore), 12 October 2007, 14.

[6] Mary Ann Hogan and George Byron Smith, *Mental Health Nursing-Reviews & Rationales* (New Jersey: Prentice Hall, 2003), 237.

[7] Sinha, 'Slapping is most common abuse', 14.

[8] National Family Health Survey, "(NFHS-3) Domestic Violence", 2005-2006. *http:// www.hetv.org/india/nfhs3/NFHS-3* Domestic-Violence. ppt (3rd October 2008)

[9] Lori L. Heise, Jacqueline Pitanguy and Adrienne Germain. *Violence against Women: The Hidden Health Burden.* World Bank Discussion Paper. (Washington D.C. The World Bank.1994), 5.

[10] https://weblearn.ox.ac.uk/site/users/manc1017/public/ipvesearch/*(accessed 15 May 2006).*

[11] Mary Ann Hogan & George, *Mental Health Nursing-Reviews & Rationales,* 2003, 237.

[12] The information and Wheel of Abuse is provided courtesy of Kim Eyer of *rhiannon3.org. www.hiddenhurt.co.uk/power_and_control_wheel.html. www.laurel.k12. mt.us/....../The_Wheel_of_Power_and_Control.pdf (accessed 5 April 2006).*

[13] Domestic Violence in India, "Physical Abuse" The protection of women from Domestic violence Acts 2005,2 *http://www. Domestic violence of India (accessed 20 July 2008).*

[14] Mary Ann Hogan & George, *Mental Health Nursing-Reviews & Rationales,* 2003, 238.

[15] Ajay Sura, "Kids forced to have oral sex at Haryana shelter," *The Times of India,* Bangalore edn.14 June 2012, 10.

[16] "What Christians Need to Know About Sexual Abuse" United News - May 2003 *http://www.ucg.org/christian-living/word-what-christians-need-know-about-sexual-abuse/* (*accessed June 10 2005*).

[17] Domestic Violence in India, "The protection of women from Domestic violence Acts 2005, "Sexual abuse" *http://www. Domestic violence of India (accessed 20 July 2008*).

[18] Domestic Violence in India, "Willful denial of sex is mental cruelty," *The Hindu* (Chennai), 22 October 2008, 5.

[19] Women in Panchayat Raj: Change agents for a new future for India. The Hunger project, "*Violence against Girls and Women*," *http://www.thp.org/sai00/India/violence.htm.* (accessed 8 February 2008).

[20] *http://www.insightandgrowth.com (accessed 20 June 2008).*

[21] *http://www.insightandgrowth.com (accessed 17 June 2007).* Article Source: *http://EzineArticles.com/1307691; http://ezinearticles.com/?expert=Dr._Laila_Ahmed.* Dr. Laila Ahmed a post graduate in psychology and master trainer for National Federation of Neuro Linguistic Psychology, Theta Healing and certified Clinical Hypnotherapist, registered with the Indian Board of Alternative Medicine.

[22] Mary Ann Hogan & George, *Mental Health Nursing-Reviews & Rationales* (New Jersey: Prentice Hall, 2003), 238.

[23] "A woman was set on fire by her husband," *Times of India* (Bangalore), 29 July 2007, 3.

[24] *Dr. Jay Grady, You are a Door Prize, Not a Doormat, (Houston, Therepia Publishing 2003),* 23-24.

[25] Ibid., 30.

[26] David Johnson & Jeff Van Vonderen, '*The subtle power of spiritual abuse*' Bethany House publishing, Minnesota, 1991.

[27] Ronald Enroth Recovery from church that abuse (Grand Rapids: Zondervan, 1994), 72-74.

[28] http:// www.Spiritual Abuse Recovery Resources.org. Jeff Van Vonderen summarizes the term ' spiritual Abuse' in the introduction to this website. *(accessed 5th July 2006).*

[29] Indian government "Dowry demands and dowry death," *http:// www.indiagov.org/social/women/legal.htm, www.indianchild.com/dowry_in_ india.htm. (accessed 10th June 2007).*

[30] Madhu Purnima Kishwar, "Destined to Fail-Inherent Flaws in the anti Dowry Legislation," *Manishi* 148 (2005), 9.

[31] "Dowry," *The Columbia Encyclopedia, Sixth ed.*, 2007.

[32] Statistics Times.com "Sex ration of India, 2015.

[33] International Institute for Population Sciences (IIPS) and Macro International. 2007. *National Family Health Survey (NFHS-3)*, Domestic Violence *2005–06: India: Volume II*. Mumbai: IIPS. *http://www.nfhsindia.org (accessed 25th April 2006)*.

[34] Social problems in independent India, "Bride burning & Dowry Death," *http; // www. Fun on the net (accessed 7 September 2007)*. NDTV.Com Dowry Laws the weakest link

[35] "Declining Child Sex Ratio of Urban Jabalpur: Challenge before the Civil Society," Christian Medical Association of India, Policy Advocacy of the CMAI, 2005. Niti.gov.in /planning commission *(accessed 6th August 2006)*.

[36] "Increasing female feticide : Challenge before Christians," Christian Medical Association of India, Policy advocacy of CMAI, 2005.

[37] Abortion, female infanticide, feticide, son preference in India, Copy right 2000. Indian child.com *(accessed 13th May 2005)*.

[38] Jonathan Abbamonte "63 million women in India are ' missing' more than 11 million are 'missing' due to sex-selective abortion" Population Research Institute, February 13, 2018.

Renuka Bisht, "21 million 'unwanted' girl, 63 million 'missing' women - Econiomic survy underlines India's gender crisis." The Time of India-Blogs 29 January, 2018.

[39] J.E.Park and K.Park, text book of Preventive and Social Medicine- A Treatise on Community Health (Jabalpur: Banarsidas Bhanot Publishers, 2007), 402.

[40] Ibid.,402.

[41] K.L. Sharma (ed), *Social Inequality in India* (New Delhi: Rawat Publications, 1999), 127.

[42] M.S.Gore, The traditional Indian family in comparative family systems, (Boston:Houghton Miffin, 19650, 216.

[43] Wikipedia, the free encyclopaedia "patriarchy," com.htm

[44] Patel, Ila. "The Contemporary Women's Movement and Women's Education in India." International Review of Education / International Zeitschrift für Erziehungswissenschaft / Revue International del' Education 44 (1998): 157. (1st April 2007).

[45] Case Study 1 Names are changed to protect the identity of the individual.

[46] Case Study 2 Names are changed to protect the identity of the individual.

[47] Case Study 3 Names are changed to protect the identity of the individual.

[48] Case Study 4 Names are changed to protect the identity of the individual *https://www.dailypioneer.com/nation/india-sees-22-dowry-deaths-every-day.html*, August 1, 2015 *(accesed 20 June 2018).*

Chapter 3

Theological
and Biblical Perspectives
on Abuse of Women

In chapter two, we saw types and the major causes for abuse of women. In this chapter, we look at the theological perspectives of Old Testament and New Testament marriage, Biblical teachings on the Christian family and equality in marriage.

Misinterpretations or wrong concept on Christian marriage, family, headship, submission and inequality can encourage abuse of women. The author deals with these concepts in detail to find possible solutions to reduce or do away with the abuse as much as possible.

Biblical Views on Abuse

The Bible strongly condemns abusive behavior of men. Marriage is for a loving, caring and long lasting relationship and not for harassment of any kind. Many passages in the Bible speak out on the issue of abuse, and God's attitude towards those who repeatedly abuse. In Psalms 11:5 it says, "The LORD examines the righteous, but the wicked and those who love violence his soul hates." The prophet in Zephaniah 1:9 says, "On that day I will punish all who avoid stepping on the threshold, who fill the temple of their gods with violence and deceit." Psalms 37:9 says, 'For evil men will be cut off, but those who hope in the LORD will inherit the land." Malachi 2:16-17 also says, "...I hate a man's covering himself with violence as well as with his garments," "…you have wearied the Lord with your words." How have we wearied him'? "…all who do evil are good in the eyes of the Lord, and he is pleased with them', or 'Where is the God of justice?"

Similarly, 'wrath' or 'anger' is condemned as being sinful, as is sexual abuse. The following are some of the Biblical examples. James 1:19, 20 "Everyone should be quick to listen, slow to speak and slow to become angry, for man's anger does not bring about the righteous life that God desires. Ephesians 5:3-5, "But among you there must not be even a hint of sexual immorality, or of any kind of impurity, or of greed, because these are improper for God's holy people. Nor should there be obscenity, foolish talk or coarse joking, which are out of place, but rather thanksgiving. For of this you can be sure: No immoral, impure, or greedy person-such a man is an idolater-has any inheritance in the kingdom of Christ and of God."

Before entering into further discussion, let us look at what the Bible says about verbal abuse. Scripture shows us that the very harsh or inhuman words we speak can be considered as a form of violence. The following Biblical passages speak about verbal abuse. Proverbs 10:6, "Blessings crown the head of the righteous, but violence overwhelms the mouth of the wicked." Proverbs 10:11, "The mouth of the righteous is a fountain of life, but violence overwhelms the mouth of the wicked." Matthew 5:21, 22, "You have heard that it was said to the people long ago, 'Do not murder, and anyone who murders will be subject to judgment.' But I tell you that anyone who is angry with his brother will be subject to judgment. Again, anyone who says to his brother, 'Raca,' is answerable to the Sanhedrin. But anyone who says, 'You fool!' will be in danger of the fire of hell."

As true followers of Christ we are encouraged to consider everything we say to one another, whether it stands the test of being for the benefit of the hearer - verbal abuse certainly does not qualify. Ephesians 4:29, "Do not let any unwholesome talk come out of your mouths, but only what is helpful for building others up according to their needs, that it may benefit those who listen." James 1:26, "If anyone considers himself religious and yet does not keep a tight rein on his tongue, he deceives himself and his religion is worthless." James 3:10, "Out of the same mouth come praise and cursing. My brothers, this should not be." Ephesians 4:31, "Get rid of all bitterness, rage, and anger, brawling and slander, along with every form of malice." These are the instructions concerning one's speech.

The Old Testament contains three specific instances of sexual abuse. The first occurrence is described in Genesis 19:30-38, involving Lot and two of his daughters. The daughters initiated incestuous relations with their father, perhaps in the mistaken belief that the entire world had been destroyed (this occurred shortly after the destruction of Sodom and Gomorrah) and they were the only humans left on the earth.

The second incident is about the rape of Dinah, the daughter of Jacob described in Genesis "Now Dinah, the daughter of Leah ... went out to see the daughters of the land. And when Shechem ,... saw her, he took her and lay with her, and violated her" (Genesis 34:1-2). In this case, it is obvious that she was raped. Unquestionably, the emotional reactions of family members toward a rape victim have not changed at all through the millennia. When Dinah's brothers heard about the rape, their reaction is seen in Genesis 34:7, "…they were filled with grief and fury, because Shechem had done a disgraceful thing in Israel by lying with Jacob's daughter- a thing that should not to be done."

Third, was the rape of Tamar, (one of the daughters of King David, who is extraordinary beautiful) by her half-brother, Amnon (2 Samuel 13). Amnon desired Tamar and he devised a scheme to get her alone with him in his house (2 Samuel 13:1-10). Once there, he asked her to lie with him. She resisted and even told him that if he wanted her, all he had to do was ask their father. She told him that King David would allow them to be married if Amnon requested. She begged him not to rape her (2 Samuel 13:11-13). In other words, his sensual desire could not be controlled hence he did not bother to take mutual consent.

In the life of Tamar we can see an unprotected or undefended woman who is being treated as an instrument of pleasure by her half brother. Her position in the narrative is the actual position of many women in our society. She hinted that the 'law' did not permit what he plotted, and also warned him of the consequences of wickedness and shameful action. The covetousness of the man however conquered him, like most of the exploiters of his times and our times. He hated her after the act and threw her out of his palace.

We hear of incidents where rapists cruelly murder the victims. Like this woman, resentment is the life experience of the people who suffer abuse. The following are the reactions of Tamar, King David and Absalom. Tamar's reaction was a distinctive one. "Tamar put ashes on her head and tore the ornamented robe she was wearing. She put her hand on her head and went away, weeping aloud as she went" (2 Samuel 13:19). This passage reveal to us her deep seated grief, shame, anguish, frustration, breach of brotherly affection, helplessness, low self esteem, and above all losing her virginity.

Many victims after a sexual attack withdraw from their previous activities and from associating with other people. The Bible does not say what happened to Tamar afterwards. Nothing much is recorded of Tamar's life after this incident but like all the other survivors of sexual violence she might have lived a lonely, resentful, and sorrowful life. King David was 'furious' (2 Samuel 13:21), but he kept the incident secret and took no direct action against Amnon. But Absalom, brother of Amnon and Tamar was extremely angry "…he hated Amnon because he had disgraced his sister Tamar" (2 Samuel 13:22). The rape of Tamar set in motion events that led to his own death at the hand of Absalom (2 Samuel 13:23-39). David's ineffectiveness led Absalom to feel angry and resentful toward his brother. Absalom chose to use his desire for revenge as an excuse for committing murder. He also felt anger towards his father for failing to protect Tamar.

The Bible warns about the dangers of an angry man. Proverbs 22:24 says, "Do not make friends with a hot- tempered man, do not associate with one easily angered" and Proverbs 29:22 says, "An angry man stirs up dissension, and a hot-tempered one commits many sins" Psalms 52:2-3, "your tongue plots destruction; it is like a sharpened razor, you who practice deceit. You love evil rather than good, falsehood rather than speaking the truth." Cruelty against a human being is sin in the sight of God.

The side effects of sexual abuse differ from victim to victim depending on the age, the type of abuse, (whether it is rape or childhood sexual assault) the brutality and cruelty as well as the extent of the abuse.

Let us look for an approach in the Bible that will release women from the bondage of marginalization, violence and exploitation. Abuse of women is a violation of Biblical principles, and also inhuman and callous behavior. God does not like violence in any form. The Bible condemns abuse or violence. King Solomon in Proverbs 3:31 says, "Do not envy a violent man or choose any of his ways...." The farsighted or perceptive husband makes his home a joyful and blessed one by taking heed of the Scripture.

The book of Hosea is devoted to using the marriage of Hosea to compare the relationship of Jesus to the church. Hosea was instructed to marry a prostitute, a befitting description of the children of Israel who moved in and out of apostasy. The church today does the same. Time and again Hosea was required to go after his wife who was engaged in adulterous, disloyal, faithless affairs or relationships and brought her back and restored her.

In Hebrews 13:4 it says, "Marriage should be honored by all, and the marriage bed kept pure, for God will judge the adulterer and all the sexually immoral." Where the spouses respect and honor each other, there is no place for abuse in the home. Spousal abuse does not show love for God. When the vertical relationship with God is right, then the horizontal relationship with others becomes better. Marriage is one of the most genuine, legitimate, beautiful, and God ordained human relationship. It is the basic foundation of any society, and also the fundamental teaching of Jesus Christ and the Christian faith. It involves social consent, generally in the form of a civil or religious ceremony, authorizing two persons of opposite sex to engage in the social institution of marriage through sexual union.

Dr. S. Radhakrishnan, the former President of India, views marriage as, "an institution devised for the expression and development of love. Its purpose is not only the generation and nurturing of children but also the enrichment of the personality of the husband and wife through the fulfillment of their need for a permanent comradeship, in which each may supplement the life of the other and both may achieve completeness."[1] In other words, he affirms that marriage is based on mutual love, commitment, mutual trust and permanent companionship. The spouses enrich each other. There is procreation and nurturing children is the key factor of marriage relationships. Through the institution of marriage they achieve completeness in life.

The modern concept of marriage differs when compared to olden times. Some want to get married but do not want any children with the excuse that they have no time or money to raise the children. Excelling in the work area, large pay pack, cozy and comfortable house, and leading a luxurious life is more important for them. Some others do not believe in marriage ceremony but live together with the pretext that in case they decide to separate there will not be any legal implications. Some others does not want any extravagant marriage ceremony whereas many want marriage ceremony to be a big affair as it takes place only once in life time.

According to the Webster dictionary, "Marriage is an institution whereby man and woman are joined in a special kind of social and legal dependence for the purpose of family and maintaining a family."[2] Marriage is a beautiful, intimate and eternal relationship shared equally by a husband and wife in the solitude of their love. It is a sanctified and God designed relationship (Genesis 1:28). Marriage is a heterosexual relationship and not homo sexual or any other contemporary invention of marriage by any human being. Heterosexual marriage is the well-accepted universal concept of marriage that goes along with the Biblical concept that, "it is a union between a man and a woman."

Biblical Views on Marriage

In order to study Biblical perspectives on the abuse of women, it is necessary to understand the Old and New Testament views on marriage. The Bible views marriage as a sacred institution.

Polygamy was practiced in the Old Testament period. Etymologically 'polygamy' means 'many marriages'. *'Polus'* means many and *'gamos'* means marriage. Polygamy was commonly practiced among the Jews. Polygamy is not group marriage.

The Old Testament presents marriage as a divine institution. Humans are created as sexual beings, consisting of male and female counterpart. This means that though men and women are sexually and functionally different, they enjoy equal dignity and importance before God. "I will make him a helper suitable for him" (Genesis 2:18).

God designed woman to be man's suitable helper, or literally, 'a helper agreeing to him'. She was not created to be man's slave, but rather his helper. The word *'ezer'* (helper) is used in the Bible for God as the helper of the needy (Psalms 33:20; 146:5); thus it does not imply that woman is an inferior being. She is equal in nature and worth, reflecting the same divine image (Genesis 1:27). Yet she is different in function, serving as a supportive helper.

In the beginning, God commanded Adam to multiply and fill the earth (Genesis 1:22; 9:1). Therefore marriage has been God's normative model of society. For descendants to multiply, marriages were multiplied and at some point men decided it would be good to have many wives.

The Old Testament gives a vivid picture of many men with multiple wives. "The first recorded polygamist was Lamech (Genesis 4:23–24). Then Esau, who despised his birthright & caused much grief to his parents by marrying two pagan wives (Genesis 26:34). God instructed the kings of Israel not to be polygamous (Deuteronomy 17:17). It is narrated about deadly sibling rivalry between David's sons from his different wives (2 Samuel 13, 1 Kings 2); and Solomon's thousand wives and concubines leading him to idolatry (1 Kings 11:1–3). Also, Hannah, Samuel's mother, was humiliated by Peninnah the other wife of Elkanah" (1 Sam. 1:1–7).[3] The only monogamous couples after the floods were Isaac and Rebekah (Genesis 24:67), Joseph and Asenath (Genesis 41:45) . The names of polygamists in Scripture include many good and righteous men faithful to God, including Lamech, Abraham, Jacob, Moses, Caleb, Solomon, and David.

Marriage is an exclusive heterosexual covenant and is a mutual relationship between one man and one woman. (Genesis 2:22-24). God created a suitable helper as a woman to Adam and not a man as a companion. Therefore, it eliminates or abolishes same sex marriages as an option (Romans 1:26, 27).

Thus, a marriage union not only fills the need for companionship, but it also enables a man and a woman to become more complete and perfect persons. The Bible compares the marriage between a man and woman as similar to the relationship between Christ and his church. Husbands are to love their wives in the same way that Christ loved the church.

We are living in an age and time where different types of marriages and relationships are very common namely monogamy, gay and lesbian marriages, live-in relationships, polygamy, and polyandry. Some marriages are solemnized in the church, some held at places convenient to the family, and some couples start to live together without having any religious ceremony. The parents, relatives, or friends may arrange marriage, 'with the consent of the man or woman' or 'arranged by the man and woman,' with or without the consent of the parents.

Polygamy is defined as, "any form of marriage in which a person may have more than one spouse at a time."[4] Polygamy means, one husband having several wives. It is a violation of the commitment inherent in marriage (1 Thessalonians 4:2-3; Hebrews 13:4).

Jesus' emphasis on the blue print of marriage from Genesis 2:24, is unconditional, permanent and monogamous. It was God's idea for humanity from Christ's teachings on marriage (Matthews 19:4-5). Monogamy "is a marriage in which there is only one wife and one husband."[5] In 1 Corinthians 7:2, the Apostle Paul teaches monogamy. He cited the creation account in Genesis 1:27 and 2:24, saying, "...and they will become one flesh." Thus we understand that violence against women is condemned in the Bible. Violation of biblical principles can lead to violence against women. In the Bible extra-marital affairs, substance abuse and adultery are condemned as being some of the reasons for violence against women. "...your body is a temple of the Holy Spirit" (1 Corinthians 6:19a). Polygamy is a violation of the commitment inherent in marriage (1 Thessalonians 4:2-3; Hebrews 13:4).

Biblical Teachings on Marriage

In order to understand theological and Biblical perspectives on abuse, one must have a clear idea about what is meant by a healthy marriage. Christian marriage is a lifelong covenant relationship between one MAN and one WOMAN to the exclusion of all others. "We believe in the covenant faithfulness of each man and woman in marriage before Jesus Christ."[6]

Marriage is considered as a holy, God-ordained institution (Genesis 1:27:2:24); it is a lifelong covenant and permanent relationship between a man and a woman until death parts them. According to Helen L. Conway, "Marriage is not just about the social union created by a couple committing themselves to each other. It is more than the physical union, which results from the act of sexual intercourse. It is also about emotional closeness. It is about mutual trust and confidence, a unique sharing of lives, hopes, and aspirations, which makes the spouse more important than one's own self."[7] Another definition of Biblical marriage is by John Stott who defines Biblical Marriage as "an exclusive heterosexual covenant between one man and one woman, ordained and sealed by God, preceded by a public leaving of parents, consummated in sexual union, issuing in a permanent, mutually supportive partnership, and normally crowned by the gift of children."[8]

The components that are essential for Biblical marriage are leaving, cleaving, and becoming one (Genesis 2:24). There are men and women who fail to build strong covenant marriages because they are still not willing 'to leave' their attachment to their parents, jobs, past lives, friends, influences, traditions, beliefs, or even church work, in order to establish strong marital relationships. The Hebrew word *Azah* means to leave, loose or discard. Leaving enables the couple to stand on their own feet without depending on their family or others. This means a change from dependency to independency. This course of action helps the newly married couple to understand each other and to practice adjustment. Leaving in a marriage is possibly the hardest choice one may ever have to make. Frequently, entering into a marriage is a stern commitment. Most people fully mean to follow through for better or worse. But there are times when it becomes apparent that it is not in the best interests of either party to stay married. If you feel you have tried every available attempt at reconciliation and it hasn't worked, it may be time. Leaving without cleaving is also insufficient.

Dabaq (Hebrew) to cling, cleave, stay, lock - 'glue'. *Kollao* (Greek): to join fast together, to glue. 'Cleaving' means a bond between husband and wife for a healthy togetherness and intimacy in their marriage relationship. 'Cleaving' reflects the central concept of covenant-fidelity. The Hebrew word for 'cleave' *dabaq*, suggests the idea of being permanently glued or joined together to something or someone. So a man is to pursue hard after his wife after the marriage ceremony (the courtship should not end with the wedding vows) and is to be .... 'stuck to her like glue'. This cleaving indicates the closeness; there should be no closer relationship than that between the two spouses, not with any former friends, relatives or with either of their own parents. The closeness must be with their spouse alone. Cleaving means, 'sticking together in thoughts, beliefs, habits, hopes, decisions, plans, and feelings and going forward with oneness and unity.' The cleaving becomes more effective if, and only if, leaving takes place ahead of it. The term 'cleaving' denotes leaving the old relationship, bonding with their new relationship and establishing a new home; wholehearted commitment which glues them permanently.

The phrase 'one flesh' needs some clarification as it is misunderstood to refer primarily to the sexual union. To become 'one flesh' (Genesis

2:24) means to become one functioning unit. H. C. Leupold explains that becoming one flesh "involves the complete identification of one personality with the other in a community of interests and pursuits, a union consummated in intercourse."[9] The term 'one flesh' means that just as our bodies are one whole entity and cannot be divided into pieces and still is whole, so God intended it to be with the marriage relationship. There are no longer two individuals, but now there is one entity, a married couple. There are a number of aspects to this new union. Emotionally, spiritually, intellectually, financially, and in every other way, the couple is to become one. It also refers to the physical or sexual aspect of marriage. Sexual desire must become the desire for the total union and oneness of body, soul, and spirit between spouses.

In Indian society due to the culture pattern, the first two factors, namely leaving and cleaving, are not fully accomplished throughout the years. In the Indian family, it is the patriarchal and patrilineal family that prevents couples from leaving and cleaving completely from their family ties or relationships. If the leaving and cleaving factors of marriage are not fully accomplished, there are possibilities of misunderstandings, suspicions, uncertainties, adjustment problems and strained relationships. Others may also interfere between husband and wife.

Views of Marriage: Traditional, God's Plan of Relationships, Modern (or Post Modern?)[10]

	Traditional of hierarchical Indian	God's Plan and Practice	(Post) Modern
Commitment	Commitment to the marriage	Covenant between partners	Contract for self-fulfillment
	Coercive	Cohesive	Disengaged
	Dutiful sex, male pleasure	Affectionate sex, mutual pleasure	Self-centered sex, personal pleasure
Adaptability	Law	Grace	Anarchy
	Pre-set, segregated roles		

		Creative, interchangeable roles	Undetermined, undifferentiated roles
	Rigid	Adaptable	Chaotic
Authority	Ascribed power	Empowering Mutual	Possessive power
	Authoritarianism, male headship		
		submissiveness, interdependence	
		Absence of authority, no submissiveness	
	Male centered	Relationship centered	Self-centered
Communication	Inexpressiveness	Intimacy	Pseudo intimacy
	Pronouncement legislation	Discussion, negotiation	Demand, stalemate
	Non/assertive, aggressive	Assertive	Aggressive

The above chart summarizes three views of marriage. Leaving the old traditions and customs, which are detrimental in one's life and cleaving to Biblical principles is highly essential for the smooth relationship. While respecting the customs and traditions of culture, one should not forget that God's plan should be accomplished in each individual.

In the traditional hierarchical system, marriage is a commitment rather than a covenant. It is also coercive. It is the choice of man. There is no place for mutual relationship. Authority is vested in the male-the central figure of marriage. Lack of openness in communication is there. Some men still defend male dominated leadership without giving enough freedom to their wives. Some men consider that a woman's body is for men's enjoyment, and that a woman's primary responsibility is to procreate, nurture the family, and to take care of family planning and the spacing of children. This is not at all true; both husband and wife have equal responsibility. Problems are compounded when there is a taboo against discussing sexuality between spouses. If traditions and customs are blindly followed, then marital problems can occur. This in turn gives way to violence against women.

Components of a Healthy Marriage

The components of a healthy marriage are mutual commitment, dedication, loyalty, effective communication, compatibility, adjustment, stewardship, equality, trust, love, care, respect, and transparency.

Marriage is a lifelong commitment between two (man and woman) not so perfect partners, based on a Biblical foundation which remains 'until death.' This means forsaking all outside influences and committing themselves to be faithful to each other until death. If either spouse has broken the commitment in the marriage, extra-marital affairs, adultery and broken relationships can happen and thus leads to abuse of women. Marriage is for the mutual fulfillment and satisfaction of both man and woman.

The success or failure of the marriage may be determined by the way in which the spouses communicate. Communication is defined as, "the sending out to someone an idea, feelings, or need in such a way that what the other person understands is reasonably identical to what you intended to say."[11] Communication is an indispensable ingredient of human contact. It is the practice of exchanging ideas, data, information, thoughts, opinion, outlook and sentimental feeling of the spouses to each other. Good communication may not happen easily, but it needs quality time, sacrifice, and obligation, effort, active listening, and patience.

Appropriate communication between a husband and wife will result in a deeper and more meaningful relationship; improved ability to solve conflicts, and a greater understanding of each other's responsibilities. The words or terminology must be the reflection of one's commitment to Christ. Therefore, the words one utters must be pleasing to God and edifying to each other. Communication should focus on sharing opinions, beliefs, concerns, emotions, needs, intimate feelings, hopes, and fears between the spouses. Factors which are essential for good communication are, to take time to know and understand each other, to be transparent, and to speak the truth in love. In contrast, communication can hurt, injure, and wound the spouse and this may lead to different forms of abuse.

The two important words to be remembered in marriage are nourish and cherish. *Ektrepho (Gk)*, means *Nourish* to rear or to bring up, care for, protect, to work for growth, development, and to support physically, spiritually, and emotionally. It means, "to provide with intellectual or emotional sustence or enrichment; sustain with food."[12]

Thalop (Gk), means cherish to appreciate, encourage and to show love and affection. To a husband the term 'cherish' should mean to love his wife as Christ loved the church. Moreover, he must make sure she has time to be alone with God, time together with his Word, also have time for each other. It means, to love and have a high regard for someone more than to love oneself. People can love, care, and show concern for each other, without cherishing one another. It is more than love, care and concern, it means to keep the other first in one's mind, value them more deeply, appreciate, being grateful or thankful for them, to treat them gently. This love will help and protect from all the deteriorating factors of marriage.

Nourishing and cherishing means mutual help, seeking the other's welfare, and comfort in the midst of prosperity and adversity in married life. The Bible gives well defined directives to cherish and nourish one's wife rather than abusing her. When inequality dominates the relationship, there is no place for mutual love and care. These trigger clashes and inferiority or superiority complexes which in turn contribute to the violence against women.

Christian Family

According to Maclver, the family is "a group defined by a sex relationship sufficiently precise and enduring to provide for the procreation and upbringing of children."[13] The family is the primary unit of human culture and society and a biological unit implying institutionalized sex relationship between husband and wife. It is a physiological and psychological union which includes procreation and nurture of children.

The Bible says, "…male and female He created them." (Genesis 1:27). While God first created man, God realized that man by himself was not complete. Therefore God said, "It is not good for the man to be alone" (Genesis 2:18). Therefore "God made a woman from the rib he had taken out of the man" (Genesis 2:21) so that through her the man might find full meaning, have completeness and fullness through companionship and love. A constant mutual fellowship is included in this companionship between man and woman. Family is very important in front of God. A family is comprised not only of husband and wife, but also the children. If the relationship between them is strained, the function of the family is not fulfilled. Due to this, unhappiness can occur. This unhappiness can build tension and pressures in life which can lead to abuse of women.

According to Chunk Smith, "While creating woman God created her with a different physical and emotional structure. Along with the physical differences, certain emotional differences were created. In the emotional realm God created the woman with a higher sensitivity than the man. His emotions move in a narrower spectrum and a woman's emotional spectrum is quite wide. She's capable of great highs; she's capable of great lows. Yes, a man can get excited and a man can get depressed. But, as a general rule, he cannot appreciate as much as a woman or enjoy himself as much as a woman."[14] Intellectually both have the same capacity but women have more understanding and appreciating capacity than most men. Therefore each one has a responsibility and accountability to build a strong family. When both of them are willing to share the responsibility, it will reduce tension and pressures on one partner. If the husband is unable to recognize and accept these responsibilities, it might cause adjustment problems which may spark the abuse of women."

Love

Love is vital to any relationship, yet many lack the quality of love God requires. The couple needs to grow in love for God and people. It should be unconditional. Love does not only receive strength from physical fellowship; it also gives the one-flesh union strength. First Corinthians 13:13b says that the greatest is love. It is because God is love (1 John 4:8); He has communicated his love to us (1 John 4:10) and he commands us to love one another (John 13:34-35). Not only must the husband be a leader but, he also must be a protector and a provider. Husbands, love your wives. The word 'love' is an agape love, which is a self-giving and self-sacrificing love. This is the kind of love that a husband needs to have for his wife.

This authentic and genuine love has the spirit of forgiving and forgetting. If love is absent in family life, selfishness creeps in. 1 Corinthians 13:4-5 says, "Love is patient, love is kind. It does not envy, it does not boast, it is not proud. It is not rude, it is not self seeking, it is not easily angered, and it keeps no record of wrongs." This is the starting point of mutual love. If this kind of love is not exercised, abuse of different forms creeps in.

According to Anne Cetas,[15] "Love will only grow when we ponder love, pray for love, and practice love." According to her we must pray for genuine love and when God hears the prayer, then we need to practice it in our relationship with others, especially in our marital relationships. We need to practice the love of Christ shown to us by our spouses also. When Christ's love grows in us, then his love flows from us in every relationship. Then there will be no chance of abuse in marital relationships.

Mutual Leadership

The husband and wife exercise different styles of leadership at home. One can observe that not all the husbands have the gift of leadership. If the husband and wife are joined in the bond of love and respect, the family will be strengthened and their relationship will be deepened. The beauty of headship at home will depend mainly on mutuality rather than individuality. Marriage is for complementing each other rather than competing and finding fault with each other. Husband's and wife's knowledge, talents, and abilities can be used for the welfare and unity of the family, also in major decision making, in raising the children, their education and choosing life partners for them. The role of the husband is not to grab the complete responsibility of controlling the home by force. The leadership qualities of the wife also should be recognized, encouraged and respected. As a result of violent behavior against women, the potential of the woman is either suppressed or masked. A couple should be grateful and thankful for each other, forgiving and forbearing with one another and leading a God centered life which helps to raise a model family.

Mutual Responsibility

Genesis 1:28b says, "...rule over the fish of the sea and the birds of the air and over every living creature that moves on the ground." This command is for both the husband and wife. Therefore, the household tasks must be shared. Both need to be good stewards of their time, money, talents, and gifts. Membership, ministry, and mission are open to all in his kingdom, based upon the personal vocation, moral and personal qualifications, and the gifts of the Holy Spirit. The husband and wife are equally responsible before God in developing a Christian home. One cannot make any excuses regarding this. They both are the partakers of the Christian home. The Bible not only mentions the wife's responsibility to the husband, but the husband's responsibility to the wife also. Both have a mutual commitment to their responsibility (Ephesians 5:22-28). The Bible not only talks about the children's obligation to their parents, but it also gives the parent's obligation to the children (Ephesians 6:1-4). "Children, obey your parents in everything, for this pleases the Lord. Fathers, do not embitter your children, or they will become discouraged" (Colossians 3:20, 21). In certain families the husband does not take up family responsibilities due to laziness, lack of proper childhood training, lack of seriousness about the family or lack of maturity. Invariably it is handed over to the wife who has to manage the family single handedly. His demands may be more, he does not understand how she is managing the finances in the family, educating the children, and socializing. It becomes an added burden if he is an alcoholic, drug addict, gambler, or an adulterer. All these factors lead to all kinds of abuse in particular, financial, social, verbal, psychological and physical.

Mutual Respect

Respect for each other is highly essential. There are plenty of differences between every couple, and in every area of their lives. They will need to forget their differences and respect each other as human beings. While respecting each other, they are to give glory and honor to the creator. They both have to respect their parents and relatives also. Mutual respect for a healthy and long lasting and permanent relationship must be developed and maintained.

Mutual Submission

Submission means, "being obedient, humble, yielding to power and authority."[16] The character of Christ is an example of inclusive obedience through absolute submission; Satan is just the opposite in nature and is rebellious. The nature of rebellion is to always revolt against the authority or good. The submission of a wife to her husband is instructed in religions like Islam, Buddhism, and Hinduism, but not in Christianity. "Biblical submission is always bonded with agape love. First of all the Christian must be submissive to God. (Ephesians 5:21, 22; 6:1, 5, 9; 1 Peter 1:17; 2:17); Christians are to be mutually submissive to each other (Ephesians 5:21; Romans 12:10; Philippians 2:1-8) in family relationships (1 Corinthians 7:3-5; 11:11; Ephesians 5:21-22; 1 Peter 3:1-7). Finally, Christians are to be submissive to all those who are in authority (1 Peter 2:13-17)."[17] Spouses must be submissive to God and to each other. Mutual submissiveness brings equality between spouses. Mutual submission is the basis for any harmonious and healthy relationship.

In Ephesians 5:21 it is written 'Subject to one another out of reverence for Christ." This shows the way for mutual submission. Submission means showing respect to each other, listening to others, learning from each other, and building up each other. Mutual submission is Christian love in action, treating each person with dignity and with the awareness that God created humans in his own image. Submission as envisioned in the Christian faith is always voluntary. Jesus teaches the ethics of self-giving and spiritual love as the true goal of Christian life. Mutual submission means, caring for others, meeting their physical, spiritual, and emotional needs. It is the obligation of all believers to respect and honor one another and to promote each other's well being (Romans 12:10-16; 15:1-2; Galatians 6:2; Colossians 3:11). Submission to each other also means understanding each other. A partner who understands and accepts the positive and negative traits of himself and his wife can never initiate violence against her.

The Bible teaches that Jesus Christ came to redeem women as well as men and that husbands and wives are heirs together of the grace of life (1Corinthians 7:3-5; Ephesians 5:21). The husband's function as 'head' *(kephale)* is to be understood as self-giving love and service within this relationship of mutual submission (Ephesians 5:21-33; Colossians 3:19; 1 Peter 3:7). Man is to be the head of woman is the same as Christ being the head of the Church. In the Old Testament, one was made the head over the people in order to lead, guide, provide and protect. Mutual submission is God's desire and aspiration and should not give the wrong impression.

In conclusion, "Biblical submission is universal submission. The Christian is first subject to God (Ephesians 5:21, 22; 6:1, 5, 9; 1 Peter 1:17; 2:17); then Christians are mutually subject to each other (Ephesians 5:21; Romans 12:10; Philippians 2:1-8). Husbands and wives are to be mutually in submission to each other (1 Corinthians 7:3-5; 11:11; Ephesians 5:21-22; 1 Peter 3:1-7). And finally, Christians are to be subject to all" (1 Peter 2:13-17).[18]

Sanctity of Life

In Christianity more emphasis is given for the value 'sanctity of life' than in any other community. For Christians, human life has a different concept because we share the nature of God in our lives. Genesis describes how "the Lord God formed the man from the dust of the ground and breathed into his nostrils the breath of life…." (Genesis 2:7). This happens only with the human and not with any other species.

Christians believe that humans have a soul, which leaves them after their death. God will judge the soul. If people have souls, then they must be treated as special beings because Almighty God created humans. Therefore, it is considered as sacred and holy.

In Psalm139:13-16, "For you created my inmost being; you knit me together in my mother's womb. I praise you because I am fearfully and wonderfully made; your works are wonderful, I know that full well. My frame was not hidden from you when I was made in the secret place. When I was woven together in the depths of the earth, your eyes saw my unformed body, all the days ordained for me were written in your book before one of them came to be."

The apostle Paul in 1 Corinthians 3:16 said, "Don't you know that you yourselves are God's temple and that God's spirit lives in you?" Again in 1 Corinthians 6:19 the apostle Paul mentions that each Christian is a temple of the Holy Spirit, therefore, the Holy Spirit is residing in him. Jesus showed in his actions and teaching that all people should be valued. "A new commandment I give to you: Love one another. As I have loved you, so you must love one another." (John 13:34).

Christians believe that when considering issues regarding life and death, abortion, illegal sex discrimination, cloning, contraception, euthanasia, and suicide, their belief in the sanctity of life should influence all their decisions. Life is a gift from God. Every gift given by him should be used in such a way as to glorify him. Violence against women is a sin as it is against the image of God. If sanctity and sacredness of life is maintained in every Christian home, then there is no place for abuse of women.

Biblical Equality

Biblical equality is the belief that all people are equal in the sight of God because God created men and women who share maleness and femaleness. Men and women have equal responsibility to use their gifts, talents and obey their calling without any discrimination on class, gender, status, or race. Biblical equality is rooted and grounded in Jesus Christ and not in any man made institutions. Equality means, the state of being in the same status and nature.

After creating man God said, "...it is not good for the man to be alone. I will make a helper suitable for him." (Genesis 2:18). God's divine plan was that man needs a suitable helper, and hence woman was taken from his own rib. This shows that woman is a part of man, not someone from another object or orbit. Without woman, man is incomplete.

In the Garden of Eden, they both received punishment equally but differently. Both man and woman are alike and yet different in their physical, psychological, emotional aspects. Because of this difference, each one is in a position to meet the other's need in every aspect. According to Alan Padgett, professor of Systematic Theology at Luther Seminary, biblical equality is equal to human equality. This simply means that all people are equal before God, in church, home, and society. Many women and men have a life long struggle for justice, equality, and peace.

Humans are made "...a little lower than the heavenly beings" (Psalm 8:5), and have equal dignity as children of God. For this reason, every human being deserves respect and love. Equality in moral, spiritual, and political realms does not mean that all people are the same. Jesus notices the difference between good and evil, between just and unjust people.

God created man first and then woman from the same man to demonstrate that she is his equal in all aspects of his life. Likewise, Adam said in Genesis 2:23a of Eve, "this is now bone of my bones and flesh of my flesh she will be called woman." Woman was created from the side of man, to be his companion, helpmate and friend. Therefore the Apostle Peter concluded in 1 Peter 3:7 "...treat them with respect as the weaker partner and as heirs with you of the gracious gift of life." This verse mainly talks about the physical rather than moral or mental strength or capacity of a female partner. From this verse many draw a wrong concept that the women are incapable. This is not true at all.

Biblical equality is deep-rooted and grounded in Jesus Christ. The truth of the Biblical equality of all persons under God is grounded in creation. According to Eichrodt, "Because man and woman emerge at the same time from the hand of the creator, and are created in God's image, the difference between the sexes is no longer relevant to their position before God."[19] It is true that men and women have equal rights. Biblical equality underlines this truth. Violation and misinterpretation of this truth by using muscle power often leads to abuse of women in Christian homes.

Opposing Views of Marriage

Headship and Submission

The patriarchal composition of the family is very common in Indian culture. The husband is considered as the head of the family, taking unilateral decisions, and controlling everything. Ephesians 5:22-23 says, "Wives, submit to your husband's as to the Lord. For the husband is the head of the wife as Christ is the head of the church." This verse is often misused or misinterpreted by saying that it is the hierarchy instructed by God and woman should be considered as man's subordinate. In other words, she is inferior to man. Man being the head, can manage the home as an autocrat. He has full control over the wife — physical, social, mental, or spiritual aspects. If the wife questions the authority or doesn't accept it, she is considered to be disobedient. It will affect the harmony of the family, leading to abuse.

"Abusive men often cite or allude to male headship and female submissiveness to justify their abuse. Ultimately, this is based on a perverted assumption of male superiority. Based on John's narrative of the Father and the Son, human male headship, is defined as harsh, authoritarian domination of an inferior or destructive heresy."[20]

As a result the violence against women is not only initiated, but also justified by misinterpreting the biblical view of headship and submission. It doesn't mean that only men are eligible for headship. He can lead, if he has the leadership skills. Moreover both the spouses have an equal role in decision making. Women's interest and importance should also be taken into consideration. Suppressing and controlling the woman by abuse and violence is done by those who are not willing to accept or recognize the potential of their wives.

Unconditional Obligation by Women

In Indian culture, more emphasis is given to adhering or clinging to the marriage even if the abuse exists and the wife has to suffer long. People fear social stigma connected with this. Romans 12:14, "Bless those who persecute you; bless and do not curse", Romans 12:17 says, 'Do not repay anyone evil for evil." Matthew 5:39b, "If someone strikes on the right cheek, turn to him the other also." Girls are taught, from early childhood, to follow the above concept and lead a life accordingly.

Women should be silent. Men think and believe that they are the decision makers in the family. Women are expected to take a subordinate role and be silent doing the household chores and rearing children. They are misinterpreting the verse written in 1 Corinthians 14:34, "women should remain silent" without understanding the reason why Paul had mentioned this. Certain denominations in Christianity strongly lay emphasis on this aspect. She suffers silently. There are strained relationships as there are many barriers for communication.

Biblical Teaching against Violence and Abuse of Women

In chapter two a brief explanation about the abuse of women and its different forms is given. This segment will furnish a Biblical view.

The challenge to understand the Bible must be taken seriously. "Scripture is always relevant, and scripture is above our tradition, our culture and our experience when it comes to matters of faith and work."[21] The Bible condemns abuse in all forms. The following are examples. In Colossians 3:19, "Husband, love your wives and do not be harsh with them." "...love your wives, just as Christ loved the Church." (Ephesians 5:25). This verse shows that it is not a one sided submission, but a mutual submission. The husband's love must be patterned after the great love of Christ for his bride (the church). The apostle Peter says, 'Husbands, in the same way be considerate, as you live with your wives, and treat them with respect."(1 Peter 3:7a) According to Gal. 3:28, women experience the saving grace of God on equal terms with men. Therefore, be faithful, protect and give honour to your wife. In Ephesians 5:21 "submit one to another." Each partner can have an appeasing attitude that will help the relationship to become stronger. Mutual submission is only possible with the power of the Holy Spirit (v18). This act is an act of submission to the Lord. 1 Timothy 3:3, "....not violent but gentle." This means to be forbearing or forgiving. Each spouse can have a peace-making attitude that will help their relationship. Only the spirit of God can bring mutual submission in one's life. According to King Solomon, violence is the behaviour pattern of wicked men (Prov. 10:6). Violence is not associated with good or godly men. Wicked men invite trouble through their lips and eventually it ruins them. In Proverbs 3:31 he compares violent men to sinners.

Ephesians 4:29, 32, 'Do not let any unwholesome talk come out of your mouths, but only what is helpful for building others up... Be kind and compassionate to one another, forgiving each other, just as in Christ God forgave you." Christians must begin to say things that will help to build or edify others. The basic Christian attitude is forgiveness. This attitude is the result of being forgiven by Christ in our lives. A person who can forgive will be kind and compassionate to others. Violence controls the mouth of the wicked (Prov. 10:11). In Psalms 37:9, we read "For evil men will be cut off, ..." Malevolent behavior is manifested in an individual who tries to take possession or control of any individual or anything. He is a manipulator.

Our parameter is Christ's love for us. Therefore, we must love one another with the love of Christ. This is the royal law, "..love your neighbor as yourself." (James 2:8). This is known as "The law of Love" which supersedes all human relationships.

The abusers as well as the abused need the spirit of forgiveness. Forgiveness does not simply mean reconciliation. There is an enormous difference between these two. Forgiveness is not denying the injury or hurt. But it is feeling the injury or hurt and releasing it by the intervention of the Holy Spirit for his glory. Apostle Paul in Ephesians 4:32 says, "... forgiving each other, just as in Christ God forgave you." This verse means that forgiving is the indispensable Christian mind-set, which is the effect of being forgiven in Christ. Therefore forgiving others is not an easy task. Even if they seek help from counselors, the power of the word of God and of the Holy Spirit is necessary for inner healing. Only God gives freedom through his Son Jesus Christ (John 8:32-36). This is a truth which leads to freedom from sin. Individuals who are under the bondage of sin cannot come out free by their own strength. However, with the power of the Holy Spirit, they can enjoy freedom.

The apostle Paul admonishes husbands, "...husbands ought to love their wives as their own bodies. He who loves his wife loves himself. After all, no one ever hated his own body, but he feeds and cares for it, just as Christ does the church-" (Ephesians 5:28, 29). Abusing or harassing one's spouse is a sin in God's sight.

According to John 10.10b, "...I have come that they may have life, and have it to the full." Getting beaten, abused, or harassed is not having fullness of life. According to the prophet Ezekiel 18:16, abuse is associated with the influence of Satan.

Injustice of Physical Abuse

It is a pattern of violent behavior that keeps one partner in a position of power over the other partner with fear, intimidation, and control. Crimes against women start even before the birth of the girl child. It is a crime to terminate the female embryo (Psalms 139:13-17; Jeremiah 1:4, 5).

The Injustice of Emotional and Verbal Abuse

The Bible condemns verbal and emotional abuse. Again Matthew 12:36, "...men will have to give account on the day of Judgment for every careless word they have spoken." All are expected to live a careful life. Every word we are using is answerable on the day of Christ's coming. Jesus said in Matthew 5:22, but anyone who says, "You fool!' will be in danger of the fire of hell." In Psalms 52:2, "Your tongue plots destructions..." Speech brings the primary evidence of an individual's character. Evil men use the tongue as the principal weapon for deceit, slander or false witness against other individuals. In the book of Proverbs, King Solomon says out of his wisdom and life experience that 'as a man speaks, so he is.'

"Do not let any unwholesome talk come out of your mouth, but only what is helpful for building others up according to their needs, that it may benefit those who listen." (Ephesians 4:29). Christians should not only avoid harmful or destructive talk, but, should also say something which helps to build or edify others. We are called to build and not to destroy others (1 Corinthians 14:3). Again v31, "Get rid of all bitterness, rage and anger, brawling, and slander, along with every form of malice." Again, Paul is saying that anger, rage, slander, and malice grieve the Holy Spirit. Therefore, we have to get rid of it.

The Injustice of Dowry System

Requiring dowry is financial abuse of women. The Ten Commandments teach us that "Thou shall not covet." (Exodus 20:17) Paying dowry for a wife is referred to in Genesis 34:12, "the price of the bride." Exodus 22:16-17; 'general law related it to social obligations." (1 Samuel 18:25; Ruth 4:3-9) there is no incident of abuse or violence in the Bible due to the dowry system. The Bible talks about bridal price in the following verses. The gift or gifts from the bridegroom to the bride (Genesis 24:22, 30, 53; Ruth 4:10; Hosea 3:2). In Genesis 24:53, "Gold given to Rebekah.' 'The costly gifts to her brother and to her mother" (Genesis 24; 53; 34:12) "The price paid to the parents." (Genesis 34:12; Ex.22:17; 1 Samuel 18:25).

To covet means to, 'desire something with a wrong motivation.' God always looks at the motives. Dowry is a gift, money, property, certain services, or anything else of value demanded and later agreed upon. According to 1 Samuel 18:23, the dowry was according to the wealth and standing of the bride or the service rendered to the parents. In Gen. 29:18, 'Jacob worked seven years for Rachel.' 'A gift from the father to a daughter was also known as dowry '(Judges 1:15; 1 King 9:16). 'David was asked to pay for Michal' (I Samuel 18:24).

The apostle Paul in I Timothy 6:10, 'For the love of money is a root of all kinds of evil.' Money is not evil, but the love and greed to acquire more money or wealth is evil. Asking for huge amounts of money or property or anything valuable is greedy behaviour. Parents are unable to get their daughters married due to dowry and other demands. The family abuses the woman until death if she has brought less or no dowry or if other daughters-in-law in the family have brought more money. Wedding gifts are acceptable in the Bible, whereas bargaining is undesirable, intolerable, and objectionable. Demanding money is covetousness.

The Unfairness of Abortion

Female feticide is a contemporary moral problem, which must be addressed. It is a serious form of violence against women as the husband or in-laws or relatives force her to abort. The reasons vary; female fetus in-utero, unwanted pregnancy, and doubts about the woman's fidelity or due to financial problems.

Abortion is wrong because of the risk to the mother's life and the killing of a human being. Female infanticide is wrong because it causes depopulation.

What does the Bible have to say about abortion and female infanticide? 'Children are recognized as a gift or heritage from the Lord.' (Genesis 33:5; Psalms 113:9; 127:3). God was seen to be the one who opens the womb and allows conception (Genesis 29:33; 30:22, I Samuel 1:19-20). The following verses prove that abortion is against God's plan and against Biblicalprinciples. One of the Ten Commandments says

"You shall not murder" (Exodus 20:13). Therefore, abortion disobeys the Ten Commandments. Deuteronomy 32:39, "…I put to death and I bring to life…" God is the final authority to decide life and death. Genesis 2:7, Life is given by God. Job 1:21, "The Lord gave and the Lord has taken away.…" Ecclesiastes 3:1-2, "…a time to be born, and a time to die." Ecclesiastes 7:17, "why die before your time." God is the giver of life and he has the full authority to give and take life.

Bearing the image of God is the essence of humanness. Luke 1:41, 44 points to the humanness of the unborn child. Psalm 51:5, Luke 1:41, 44 reflect on the scriptural view that unborn children are spiritual, rational, and moral beings. God gives life, and only God has the authority to take it. So the abuse of abortion of the female fetus is sinful and against the Bible.

Theology of the Present Generation

There are a lot of misconceptions, delusions, about marriage and family. By understanding the theology of the generations one can address these misconceptions. "Christians, and probably many others, understand that none of these alone is a good reason for a marriage, and some of the reasons show manipulation of family members, especially of women and girls. It also shows that in many people's thinking marriage is motivated by economic calculation, by control from one generation to the next, and by the view that the young woman has become a member (or property) of the young man's family, with no reciprocity towards her family. She must give birth to a son and is considered to henceforth work solely for the advantage of the males and the senior females of her new family."[22]

Families have a role to play in any society. The family is the first institution designed by God in history. It is also a nucleus of all other social groups. The functions of the family are to regulate sexual behavior, control and care for children and to offer physical, emotional, and financial security. There are two types of families in our society, namely the nuclear (conjugal) family which "is based on love and affection between the husband and wife. It consists of husband and wife and their unmarried children."[23] And the extended (joint) family which is a group of related people who generally live under one roof. Both types of families have merits and demerits. The main advantages of the extended family are financial support, rendering help to each other, opportunity for leisure, social values etc.

The patriarchal and matriarchal systems are in existence in India. However the younger generation looks forward to egalitarianism. They list the benefits of open channels of communication; it fosters an environment of equal opportunity and encourages them to strive harder. The term egalitarianism means the joint venture by the spouses in every activity, mutuality in decision-making, regulating the family resources, and child rearing. They follow the principle of equality in their family life. Dr. Howard Cline Bell, Professor of Pastoral Psychology and Counseling, in his book 'Basic types of Pastoral care and Counseling' has mentioned that equality in marriage is more enriching and has high potential and is more fulfilling for both the spouses. Traditionally the son carries on the family name and performs the funeral rites. According to theologian Steven Tracy, 'The concept of male headship' first entered the church through the Apostle Paul. This is recorded in 1 Corinthians 11:3; Ephesians 5:23. St. Paul also states that the husband is head of the wife as God the Father is head of Christ, in 1 Corinthians 11:3. Tracy interprets New Testament teaching on the subject in a way similar to many other modern Christian theologians in a variety of traditions. He points to John 5:18-24 repeatedly emphasizing that the relationship between God the Father and God the Son is one of intimate love. "Be subject to one another out of reverence for Christ." (Ephesians 5:21) "Although strong patriarchal tendencies have persisted in Christianity, the example of Christ carries the seeds of their displacement by a more symmetrical and respectful model of male-female relations."[24]

The Oregon State University sociologist Sally Gallagher interviews evangelical men and women across the country and across the denominational spectrum and concludes that "most evangelicals are pragmatically egalitarian."[25] Theoretically, evangelicals considered 'headship' only as an idea, but practically decisions are made in homes through the process of discussion, negotiation, mutual respect, love, submission, concern and consensus rather than dictatorship. However, in India most of the Evangelical homes have maintained a system of 'tradition', and some homes a system of 'conservatism'.

The Church of England aptly said. We are living in the New Testament period; we need to closely observe the teachings of Christ. Christ is expecting from us the model of care, love, concern, and respect. We need to be a role model to other families surrounding us.

Abuse of women is a matter of great concern. Fear or rejection of abuse is an important factor in the lives of most women. It determines what they do, when they do it, where they do it, and with whom they do it. Fear of abuse is a cause of women's lack of participation in activities beyond the home, as well as inside it. Within the home, women may be subjected to physical and sexual abuse as punishment or as culturally justified acts. These acts shape their attitude to life, and their expectations of themselves.

Some abusers are psychopaths or sadist. And some others simply hate their partners. Most abusers are selfish. Some abusers abuse their partner because they are misogynists having ill-feelings and hate against the opposite sex, developed from their childhood.

Endnotes

[1] Ram Abuja, *Indian Social System,* Marriage in India unit 2- Introduction (Jaipur & New Delhi : Rawat Publications, 1993), 27-28.

[2] Webster's Seventh New Collegiate dictionary, 1971, "Marriage," 518.

[3] David B. Brinkerhoff and Lynn K. White, *Sociology* (New York: West Publishing Co, 1988), 338.

[4] Norman L. Geisler, *Christian Ethics: Options and issues,* (Grand Rapids: Baker Book House,1989), 280-281. & Gleason L Archer, *Encyclopedia of Bible Difficulties,* (Michigan: Grand rapids: Zondervan, 1982), 121-124.

[5] Brinkerhoff and White, *Sociology,* 338.

[6] 2009 The Evangelical Christian Church in Canada (Christian Disciples) News, 2005-JUN-20, *http://www.cwnews.com.* "Stew" posting a response to *"Dispatches from the Culture Wars"* bulletin board on the topic *"Canada paves the way for gay marriage,"*

on 2004-DEC-09. *http://www.stcynic.com/* we do not know the creator of this image. If you are that person and would like to be credited with authorship or would like to have the image removed, please send us an Email. You can use the "contact us" button below *(accessed 15 June 2009).*

[7] Helen L. Conway, *Domestic Violence and the church* (UK: Paternoster, 1998), 45.

[8] John Stott, *Issues facing Christians* Today (Bombay (Mumbai): Gospel Literature Service, published by Marshall Morgan & Scott, 1984), 272.

[9] H. C. Leupold, *Exposition of Genesis- Volume I.* (Michigan: Grand Rapids, Baker Book House, 1977), 137.

[10] Jack Balswick, Judith Balswick, & Judith K. Balswick, *The Family: A Christian Perspective on the Contemporary Home* ([n.p.]: Baker Academic, 2007), 80.

[11] Grace H Ketterman, *Understanding your child's problems,* (Michigan: Fleming H. Revell, 1992), 31.

[12] DK Illustrated Oxford Dictionary, "Nourish," (*New York :Oxford University Press,* 2008), 559.

[13] Vidya Bhushan and D.R. Sachdeva, *An introduction to sociology,* (Allahabad: Century Printers, 1998), 285.

[14] Chunk Smith, "Christian Family Relationships," *http:// www.calvarychapel. com/ library / smith chuck /books/cfr.htm* (12 July 2008).

[15] Anne Cetas became a follower of Jesus in her late teens after a friend invited her to a Bible conference. At 19, she began reading *Our Daily Bread* and studying RBC Ministries 'Discovery Series booklets.' Six years later, she joined the editorial staff of Our *Daily Bread.* Anne began writing for the devotional booklet in September 2004 and became managing editor in 2010. Anne and her husband work as mentors in an inner-city ministry.

[16] DK Revised & Updated Illustrated Oxford Dictionary, 2008, "Mutual Submission", 829.

[17] Bob Deffinaugh, "Taking a second look at submission", *http:// www.bible.org. (accessed 10 May 2008).*

[18] Bob Deffinbaugh was more convinced than ever that the meaning of the term Peter used here is "creature," not "institution" (NASB) or "ordinance" (KJV). The term is found 19 times in the King James Version of the New Testament. It is rendered "creature" 11 times, 6 times it is rendered "creation," "building" once in Hebrews 9:11 (which the NASB changes to "creation"), and "ordinance" one time here in 1 Peter 2:13. The normal translation would thus be either "creation" or "creature." "But why," someone might ask, "does Peter use this expression

for people?" In that day, as in our own (I speak of the unborn), not all human beings are considered as such. Just as the unborn fetus has been judged to be a non-person by the Supreme Court, so slaves and others (such as the outcasts in India) are considered non-persons. Since Peter requires us to submit to every human being, he must carefully choose his words to include every divinely created human being. His expression, "human creation" does this, perhaps better than any other.

[19] Walter Eichrodt, *Theology of the Old Testament, trans. J.A. Baker, 2 Vols.* (Philadelphia: Westminster Press, 1967), 126.

[20] Steven Tracy, "Headship with a Heart: How Biblical Patriarchy actually Prevents Abuse". *Christianity Today*, February 2003.

[21] Lynn Smith, *Women, Worth and Scripture: What Does the Bible really Teach?* (Bangalore: SAIACS Press, 2005), 25.

[22] Beulah Wood, A theology of generations, 1.

[23] C.M. Abraham, *Sociology for Nurses* (Chennai: B. I. Publications, 1999), 183.

[24] The Archbishops' Council. *Responding to Domestic Abuse: Guidelines for those with pastoral responsibilities,* (Church House Publishing, 2006), 19. *http://www.cofe.anglican. org/info/papers/domesticabuse.pdf. (accessed 10 May 2006).*

[25] Sally K. Gallagher, *Evangelical Identity and Gendered Family Life* (New Brunswick, NJ: Rutgers University Press, 2003), 103.

Chapter 4

The Role of Clergy and the Church in Preventing Abuse of Women

From the Bible we have come to realize that abuse against women is not a new concept or new generation idea, but it is as old as human history itself. As days go by the abuse becomes more and more complicated. Statistics reveal that physical, psychological and verbal abuses are considered to be the highest and most common forms of abuse of women. It is a criminal offence. It damages the victim's confidence and her self-respect   to live for tomorrow by attacking her strength, ability, talents and self-esteem.

This chapter focuses on the task of clergy and the church as a community of believers to reduce or prevent abuse of women in India, especially in Christian families. The main purpose is to acknowledge and bring about awareness of the present scenario where churches do not address the abuse of women as expected. Clergy and the members of the church differ in their views regarding this issue. Both are expected to help each other and work together towards one goal- to reduce or prevent the abuse of women, especially in Christian families.

In our society men are also victims of abuse from women. But majority of cases women are victims of abuse more than men. All types of abuse have long lasting effects on the victim, even after the incident. These effects are manifested in different ways in different individuals. It influences the ability of better parenting, effectiveness in work area, and on the outlook on life. It even depressingly affects their day to day performance. Her family life becomes disordered; feelings of guilt, shame, inner pain and humiliation are additional factors. The past experiences and memories of the abuse lead her to confusion in many areas, loss of identity, and over reaction. All these lead her to a form of helplessness and defenselessness in many ways in her private family life and in her public life in church and community.

The Role of Clergy

Abuse of women and its reduction or prevention needs a joint effort by concerned individuals, the church; clergy, Christian counselors, Christian leaders, lay leaders, NGO's, institutions, women's groups and other like-minded organizations committed to reduce or prevent the abuse of women.

The clergy's role in responding to abuse is perhaps more of a frustrating and provoking job than any other service he renders. However, most of the time the clergy may be the first person a victim will contact for immediate help; he can have an important and influential role in helping people living in abusive situations. Clergy have the responsibility of keeping church and society morally incorrupt, spiritually strong and socially relevant. Therefore clergy have an outstanding role to play in dealing with the concern of abuse.

There are three broad categories of pastoral activities namely caring, teaching and advising, shepherding the flock. Teaching from the pulpit on Sundays or weekly meeting or prayer meetings, house visits, pastoral care are the other major pastoral activities. To teach means, "to impart information or skill so that others may learn."[1] The clergy must teach the word of God practically, effectively and constantly, so that changes can take place in the life of others, especially in the lives of abusers. The spiritual food provided by the clergy to his flock comes from the Word of God. To distribute the Word of God faithfully, meaningfully, and practically he must be a man of prayer and a man under the influence and guidance of the Holy Spirit. This has a nurturing and edifying value. The characteristic of bad shepherds is explained in Ezekiel 34:4, "You have not strengthened the weak or healed the sick or bound up the injured. You have not brought back the strays or searched for the lost." Clergy, 'the Shepherds' feed the flock through the ministry of preaching, teaching and counseling. Keeping the flock safe and secure from the enemies of the gospel is fundamental to the pastoral ministry and is accepted by teaching Christian doctrine faithfully without bending it to the fashion and fads of the age. According to Titus chapter 1:9, the clergy must be qualified to "…hold firmly to the trustworthy message as it has taught, so that he can encourage others by sound doctrine and refute those who oppose it." Sound doctrine here means correct biblical teaching. There is no adulteration in any manner. This covers the whole range of activities connected with structure, style, direction and discipline of the flock. He should know his people in the congregation personally and closely so that he can identify abuse in his parish and take necessary steps to reduce it without much disturbance and publicity.

Preaching and Teaching

Clergy must teach about responsibility, accountability, inter-personal relationships, developing self-control, self-discipline, consistent prayer life, forgiveness, reconciliation, effectiveness and transparency in communication, how to live according to their commitments, appreciating each other, showing reverence, respect and admiration to the partner, leading to a healthy, purpose oriented and meaningful family life.

By addressing abuse within the marital relationship openly and directly, clergy should uphold the sanctity of the marriage relationship. According to Webster's dictionary, Sanctity means the quality of being holy. Keeping the sanctity is through the ability to love, mentally, spiritually, and physically. Sanctity means keeping the companionship and the togetherness between the spouses in a holy manner. In such a relationship both of them should be transparent to each other.

Biblically, the heterosexual relationship is considered as holy and legally binding. The sanctity of the marriage loses its sheen at the first instance of abuse. Sanctity in marriage can be lost if the husband marries the woman only for financial security, social status, as a cure for mental illness, for doing household work and for biological needs alone. He should perceive her as a partner and companion who has equal rights. The husband and wife are enriched and perfected by mutual love, care and understanding. By taking action against continued unfair treatment and oppression, he must speak for a relationship that honors individual worth, security and mutual respect.

Clergy should rebuke the wrong deeds of the wrong doers especially among their own parish members or the individuals who are known to him personally; he must lovingly and gracefully rebuke the abuser irrespective of his position in church or society. "Speak the truth in Love" (Ephesians 4:15). This simply means that to rebuke him truthful and loving manner, and not putting down as an individual. In Proverbs 27:5, "Better is open rebuke than hidden love." Jesus said to his disciples in Luke 17:3, "If your brother sins, rebuke him, and if he repents, forgive him." There are plenty of incidents where Jesus rebuked disciples and others when they did wrong which are found in scripture. Many times those who do it honestly face resentment or unpleasantness. Clergy who do not correct the mistakes of wrong doers fear that they will lose popularity as they want to be in the good books of the congregation. Clergy must always remember that they are servants of God and not of men. Therefore they need to please and are accountable to the Master first; a clergy is expected to please God rather than men.

Pastoral Care

The word 'care' is derived from the Latin word *cura*,[2] which has an extensive meaning. Effective caring requires the ability to assess the different areas of need. Caring must include empathetic and compassionate elements. The clergy must take time to listen actively to the people. For this the clergy needs patience and a willingness to help others. Time and a suitable place are essential for active listening.

There may be apprehension that if secular community resources are accessed, the victim will be counseled to leave the relationship. However, within the marriage relationship the values of individual dignity, security of person and mutual respect should be paramount. When abusive behavior by one partner is used against the other, these values are disavowed and the victimized partner is violated and devalued.

Pastoral Counseling

Pastoral counseling refers to counseling in the context of the church. "Counseling skills can be used effectively in many caring situations, leading to more attentive and sensitive listening, seeing themselves specifically as counselors."[8] It is a most effective and safe method. Therefore clergy have a great role to use this as an effective method, so that others will be benefited in many ways.

Counseling is a good tool to reduce or eradicate marital abuse. It gives a chance to meet each spouse individually. Therefore, it gives ample time to collect the valuable information which is needed for the solution to the problem. A good counselor will search for the root problem through all collected data and try to investigate it. Presenting problems and the root problems are entirely different in many counseling situation. After several separate sessions, with the abuser and the abused, call them for a joint session if the time permits or willing to conduct peaceful session. At the counseling session the real counselor expert is the Holy Spirit. It is better to sort out the problems earlier than later. Counseling is a one to one relationship, to understand the problems in different situations.

Counseling should be provided at the right time (as early as possible) and at the right place. Counseling the couple together at the first session is not advisable. The partner who has an abusive behavior may defend himself with various excuses. It is effective and better to have individual counseling during times of unforgiving and cruel violence. If the preliminary counseling session goes well, then after the second or third sessions it is advisable to call them for a joint session of counseling.

During the counseling sessions, it is important to emphasize the theology of forgiveness, ministry of reconciliation and fundamental beliefs of Christianity in regards to Christian home, family, marriage, marital relationship and abuse. Forgiving and forgetting is a good medicine to avoid further abuse in the marital relationship. Apostle Paul mentioned to the Colossian people. "Bear with each other and forgive whatever grievances you may have against one another. "Forgive as the Lord forgave you" (Colossians 3:13). Here the apostle Paul is exhorting the person who has been wronged to forgive the wrongdoer whoever he may be. Forgiveness is to let loose one's bitterness towards the offender as Christ forgave us. It is good for a lifelong, happy relationship with two forgiving partners. The abuser and the abused should be encouraged to forgive each other as a part of the healing process inwardly and outwardly. The important lesson that needs to be taught is to forgive and forget for the sake of a better family and home. Clergy must use various steps with regard to forgiveness as described in Matthew 18:10-25.

Providing Support for the Victim and Family

When dealing with the abuse of women, the safety of the victim and her children must be the first priority. Abuse within an intimate relationship always has the potential to become fatal. A clergy may struggle to uphold the sanctity of marriage while addressing domestic abuse by ensuring the safety of the victim. He must be aware of the outcome, seriousness and depth of the issue, to provide adequate and timely help, to provide love, concern, mercy, compassion, and comfort, to provide immediate medical attention and teach against the abuse based on Biblical principles. Not only women, but also their families suffer in one-way or other from the repercussion of the abuse.

Domestic abuse is a difficult subject to address, not only by the church, but also by other social agencies as a whole. There are many facets that need to be considered and a range of services to be provided. It also has long-term implications for all who are affected. This highlights the need for regular home visits. In this era clergy do not have adequate time for families due to other church related commitments and responsibilities. Therefore under the supervision and guidance of the clergy, assistant clergy, the members in the women's fellowship and the elders in the church should provide guidance for the well-being of the victim and their family members.

If the number of members increases in the parish, it becomes difficult for the clergy to spend adequate and quality time with each family due to distance, working conditions, and non-availability at home during the day. This can be dealt with in many ways. Assistant clergy, elders of the church and spiritually qualified senior citizens can be appointed for assisting the senior clergy. If so, they should work as a team, apart from doing it individually. Another way is planting another parish so that the clergy and the church can strive hard to bring harmony, peace and love among the people. The support for the victim is possible when the congregation is smaller.

Constant moral support for the victim is needed to a great extent because of isolation, rejection, denial; this is the experience of the families affected by abuse or violence. The abusing partner may intentionally block the victim from being with friends, families and at social events. The victim may feel that the congregation will not accept her. Children also learn to keep the family secret as they are strictly warned not to share anything with others. There is fear of alienation and shame. The individual who has abused may feel ashamed and feel guilty for his actions. The victim of abuse may be in need of assistance, may share about the abuse experience. They can be encouraged to seek specialized assistance or counseling. Clergy should strive to create an environment where the family lives without any fear, intimidation, shame or humiliation. This cannot happen in a day or two, but with constant guidance and encouragement it may become possible.

It is easy to be impatient with a victim who seeks help. The victim may be in a state of despair, misery, hopelessness, anxiety or fear. She may not be able to talk or reveal her problems fully, the way she wants to do. The clergy may have less time to spare, so it is essential for an experienced clergy to understand her and create a suitable environment for her to be at peace. It is very important not to 'give up' on her and her situation. Women who experience family abuse will often state that they do not want to end the relationship but they want the abuse or violence to stop permanently and the victim holds on to the hope that the abuse will eventually end. The victim wants an everlasting ceasefire. Understanding some of the dynamics about domestic abuse allows the clergy and congregational members to take a 'long-term' view. It is critical for the victim to know that support is available, whenever she chooses to access it. It is also important for those who become the support for family members to be supported themselves. Another important role of the church is to bring the abuser under the Lordship of Christ. He must be tackled in the right manner so that he understands why and where he went wrong. He can be counseled and brought back to normal behavior by not condemning him; but strongly condemning his wrong deeds.

Provide Protection for the Victim and Family

The Bible makes it very clear that God hates abuse and calls clergy and other spiritual leaders to be assertive in protecting the victim if she is abused (Proverbs 2 4:11-12, Isaiah 1:17, Jeremiah 22:3). The overall protection of abused women definitely includes encouraging, supporting and isolating them from abusive husbands in a safe and secure place. Jesus pronounced the most severe judgment on those who cause one of the little ones to stumble (Matthew 18:1-10). Dr. Bruce Perry, one of the best neurological trauma researchers in the world, has commented that, "when young children merely witness domestic violence, this trauma exposure creates long-term physiological changes, including permanent structural alteration and damage to the brain."[4] Abusive husbands can cause tremendous long-term physical, emotional, and spiritual damage to the victim and other members of the family.

Sometimes the man who is abusing his wife has a childhood history of abuse from the members of the family. The girls who grow up in abusive homes have the emotional damage of childhood abuse. All of these show that growing up in an abusive home, especially physically abuse ones is extremely damaging long-term and certainly 'causes little ones to stumble.' Also the children have instability at home. Timely separation from an abusive husband is ethically very important for the wellbeing of the woman and children long term. Scripture does not commend enduring suffering. Christ repeatedly avoided physical assault by hiding (John 8:59), by maintaining physical separation from his abusers (Mathew 12:14-15, John 11:53-54), and by eluding them (John 10:31, 39). Paul and David also repeatedly fled physically abusive civil and religious authorities (1 Samuel 19:12, 27:1; Acts 9:22-25, 14:5-6, 17:8-10, 14).

Hurdles Faced by Clergy

Clergy are called by God for a special task to continue his public ministry on this earth. They are expected to teach, preach, heal, and counsel people. Unfortunately, due to various reasons, they are unable to meet the expectations of the people. Problem solving is one of the expected roles of clergy. Many fail to accomplish this role as they do not recognize at existence of problems or find it difficult to root out the problem; or are incapable of solving it due to lack of experience and skills. Some of the important hurdles faced by clergy are given below.

Insufficient Training

There is no adequate theological training for clergy to handle the crisis or abuse of women in the family and in the church. What are the measures they have to take to handle the situation? Therefore most of the clergy do not have any idea what to do and what not to do. Young inexperienced clergy need guidance and proper training in this aspect.

A few seminaries, Bible colleges, and religious study centers have prepared curriculum about prevention of abuse of women, however they do not have much emphasis in teaching this subject effectively. If in the seminaries a lot of focus is given on the issue, then it would equip to firefight and douse the problems in an amicable manner along with biblical truth.

Some clergy have good Christian family background and have never seen or heard about abusive behavior in families. Therefore, they are ignorant about the abuse. They are too inexperienced to sense the issue of abuse.

Another group of clergy often feels that they are capable of solving marital problems in people's lives. Some think they have solutions or readymade answers for every problem people face. This is not always real or true. Traditionally, clergy lived a life of solitude and depended on spiritual resources. Clergy and other spiritual leaders may distrust secular counseling, or using secular principles integrated with Biblical principles, therefore they are reluctant to make referrals to secular agencies and experts. Sometime if we cannot handle the situation, it is advisable to refer to someone who can help the victim. The victim expects a solution to their problems. Who solves the problem is immaterial for them.

Case Story 1

This incident took place in the life of a young clergy.[5] Mr. J completed his bachelor's degree in psychology with good marks and joined a theological seminary. Later he was ordained as a clergy in a well-known church in India and was posted as an assistant clergy with his basic knowledge on psychology. Rev. J was very much interested in specializing in pastoral counseling.

One day a couple came with marital problems. With much enthusiasm Rev. J decided to counsel the couple. He directly asked the question to the husband enquiring when the problem started. The furious husband jumped from his chair raging with anger and frustration and attempted to throttle his wife; he answered that it was since the time they got married. Rev. J was startled at his reaction. Due to his inexperience he was unable to handle the situation further. He had to seek help from the senior clergy to intervene and bring an immediate restoration. From then on Rev. J decided not to counsel people with marital problems. Counseling for marital problems is not a simple matter. One needs to handle it with much care and prayer.

If we look very closely at this incident, we can understand that Rev. J was young, enthusiastic, untrained and inexperienced in marital counseling. His first question itself proves his lack of experience even though he had studied psychology. He met the spouses together when the abuser was in an aggressive and hostile mood. He was over confident; probably he might have thought that with the academic backing of theology and psychology and being a clergyman he could solve all the problems of this couple.

Case Story 2

Here is another story of a clergy who had fifteen years of experience in pastoral ministry and counseling.[6] He was active in parish work and had received special training in counseling. People who came to him for counseling were very happy about his counseling as they experienced changes in their lives. Knowingly or unknowingly one day while preaching, he included some confidential matters shared during the counseling sessions as an illustration in his Sunday sermon. Many people could identify whose problem the clergy was sharing. Some people decided not to share any matters with the clergy as he cannot keep the matters in confidence. They concluded that he never kept things confidential and therefore he could not be trusted anymore and they stopped going to him for counseling or sending others to him for counseling. This clergy violated the ethical principles of maintaining confidentiality. This was either due to over-confidence or absent-mindedness.

Lack of Adequate Information about the Abuse

The nature and depth of abuse is very difficult to trace or to detect. Therefore, many times men deny the occurrence of abuse. The victim may have difficulty to explain, due to lack of proper proof, the amount of pain and agony they have experienced psychologically, emotionally, physically, spiritually, and socially. Therefore, it is very difficult to find out when, where, how, or why the abuse took place.

Theological Perplexity

One of the most challenging aspects clergy come across with the abuse of women is societal, cultural, and religious rationalization for abuse.

Families experiencing domestic abuse are often grappling with their own thinking of spiritual or religious backgrounds. Misinterpretation of the Bible and wrong Biblical teachings can influence one's life for abuse. A young husband, who believes wrong Biblical teachings, blindly starts to abuse his wife and rationalize his deeds accordingly. This may be due to lack of Biblical knowledge regarding the marriage, home and family, the role of husband and wife in regard to male headship and female submission, child rearing and managing the home. The male dominated society and its influences or aggressive nature of women can also lead to abuse of women.

Clergy can be Prejudiced

Sometimes the clergy is biased in his views regarding the abuse of women. Without having any proper information the clergy feel that husband is abusing his wife due to her fault as she is a nagging, irritating or rebellious nature. Usually she is advised not to nag or irritate him, satisfy her husband in every area of his life, be patient with him, to obey him and to fast and pray. The clergy makes her feel guilty for being the cause of abuse, as she is not submissive. He further advises the woman to stay with her husband despite abuse. She should never think of leaving him until death parts them. But the clergy did not find a solid solution to her problem of abuse. The clergy need to address the issue. If he is unable to help them find a solution, then he could have declined rather than giving wrong counsel and allowing her to go through more suffering mentally and physically.

We have seen the excuses of clergy for not addressing the issue of abuse. With proper and adequate training at the theological college, based on correct Biblical teachings, the author believes that the abuse of women can be reduced in Indian Christian families.

The Responsibility of the Church

The local church has a responsibility to hold abusers accountable and to help victims. Firstly, the Church as whole, collectively and individually, has a responsibility to offer comfort and help to those who are abused by their partner. The abusive women need a sense of reassurance, support and protection in life. The following passages may help to uplift the abusive. In Isaiah 1:17, "learn to do right! Seek justice, encourage the oppressed, defend the cause of the fatherless, plead the case of a widow." Genesis 42:21, "...surely we are being punished because of our brother. We saw how distressed he was when he pleaded with us for his life, but we would not listen; that's why this distress has come upon us." Galatians 6:2, "Carry each other's burdens, and in this way you will fulfill the law of Christ." Hebrews 12:12, "Therefore, strengthen your feeble arms and weak knees."

Secondly, the church has the responsibility to hold the abuser accountable, and to encourage the abuser to change his or her abusive behavioral pattern. Romans 15:14, "...my brothers, that you yourselves are full of goodness, complete in knowledge and competent to instruct one another." James 5:19, 20, "My brothers, if one of you should wander from the truth and someone should bring him back." 1 Thessalonians 5:11, "...encourage one another and build each other up, just as in fact you are doing."

Thirdly, the manner in which the abuser is to be admonished. Our aim is not to condemn the person, but to condemn the actions. Jesus loves the sinners and hates the sin. Therefore, we need to encourage him to repent and change his ways. 2 Thessalonians 3:15, "Yet do not regard him as an enemy, but warn him as a brother." Galatians 6:1, "Brothers, if someone is caught in a sin, you who are spiritual should restore him gently. But watch yourself, or you also may be tempted."

The active role of the local church as a community is very great with regard to reducing abuse of women. The congregation must learn about domestic violence and should let the victims know that the church is concerned about the problems or difficulties they face. The churches should not keep the fact of abuse under cover and deny that no forms of abuse are present in their respective parishes. Make it clear that abuse in the families is unacceptable in the sight of God because the purpose of God ordained marriage is love and companionship. Create an atmosphere of openness and support for the victims. Encourage church members to become involved in assisting the victims.

In India, most churches play a passive role or do nothing at all to respond to the issue of abuse of women. Some churches have the view why to get involved in this matter, what may be the outcome. Clergy often forget that healthy families constitute healthy churches. In the present day, our churches are getting filled with sick families (divorce, separation, inter- religious marriages.) While certain denominations, organizations, and leaders have proactively addressed family violence, others have ignored it and have given less priority.

The Need to Empowerment

Empowerment is the main goal to be accomplished in the powerless or weaker individual. It is not an easy task, to be attained in a day or two, but it is a continuous process. One needs to work towards the goal slowly and steadily, in a systematic manner. Empowerment comes first from the inner resources of an individual and finally it is shown in the outward behaviour and attitude. The inward power refers to the following: self-actualization, self-possession, self-assurance, self-awareness, self-acceptance, self-respect, self-appreciation, safety, security and boldness. That does not mean one is selfish.

"Empowerment is the process of challenging existing power relations and gaining greater control over the sources of power."[7] Therefore, it is a process of joint endeavor. It can be achieved by giving appropriate education, providing adequate employment, building self-confidence, enhancing a sense of equality, and fighting against sex discrimination. Empowerment should start from the grass root level; that is, at the home itself. From there it can be transmitted to the local church and then to the society at large.

Women's empowerment is said to be important for reasons of both principle and pragmatism. "It's the right thing to do because women have the same rights as men, but it's also a necessary thing to do, because it will make the world a better place and help us attain human development."[8] Never suppress their individuality due to the reason that they are born as women. The gifts and talents God has given to individuals are irrespective of sex, race or color. We need to allow them to grow physically, spiritually, and emotionally.

The empowerment of women is indispensable in the process of the development of church and society. If women are more assertive, abuse can be prevented to a certain extent. To make them bolder and financially more independent, there is a great need to empower women. This responsibility is not only for the church and the clergy but also for society, including the men. Providing education, awareness and support from the church are essential factors in empowerment.

In addition to threats to life, financial stress, and isolation, many victims are afraid of what their neighbours, friends, relatives and members of their congregation will say about them if they leave the spouse or report the abuse. If they have courage and support from society, abusee need not be suffered in silence anymore.

Once abuse is recognized, then the congregation should be in a position to offer adequate support and acceptance without any reservation to each family member. Empowering women in all aspects should be the long term goal of the clergy and the church. This will assist in restoration, reconciliation, revival and strengthening the victim and the family.

"The Government of India declared 2001 as Women's Empowerment Year (WEY). The purpose of the declaration is not to celebrate women exclusively in the new millennial year, but to make every effort to restore to woman as 'Shakti', the 'Power' that she had lost over the years in a world of growing male supremacy."[9] In other words, the year 2001 was to be the pioneer in the continual empowerment of every woman in India, at home and in the outside world. The Constitution of India protects the equality of women and empowers the State to adopt measures favorable to women. Also it imposes a fundamental duty on its citizens to defend the dignity of women.

During the public ministry of Christ, He empowered women through accommodating their needs and including their participation.

Through this gesture, he showed a marvelous example to the world around him. Jesus chose Mary Magdalene to be the carrier of the astonishing news of 'his resurrection' to his disciples. Even after two thousand years the church is still struggling to understand how the essential role of women should be carried out in the ministry.

Empowerment is an active process which enables women to realize their identity, self-worth, value, talents and gifts in all aspects of life. Empowerment helps "change their idea about the causes of their powerlessness; when they recognize the systemic forces that oppress them, and when they act to change the conditions of their lives."[10] It also means giving women power to make their own individual and independent decisions as much as they can. It enables men to see that they are using their power wrongly or sinfully to force other humans. It also refers to the day to day material needs, which must be met in order for women to fulfill their social and spiritual roles like mother, wife, and caregiver.

Empowerment is a multifaceted, multi-dimensional and multi-layered concept. Through empowering women, they gain greater share of control over the available resources, knowledge, information, ideas and financial resources, access to finances and control over decision-making in the home, church and society. "Assertiveness is saying what you want, clearly, and keeping to it without getting angry."[12] Assertiveness can help women to think and sort out the issue of abuse in a proper manner without agitating or provoking her husband or his family members. The outward appearance of women may not reveal fully all the emotional turmoil she is undergoing, whereas her inner life can be a wreck. This must be realized, understood and recognized by the church and the clergy. It is the responsibility of the church to lead the abused women in the light of the word of God and to empower her with the power of the Holy Spirit "…the truth will set you free." (John 8:32).This means freedom from the bondage of sin in every ugly manifestation. Through greater participation, women will have opportunities to see, join, speak, and learn to do things for themselves.

Empowering women includes improving the participation of women in different sectors rather than suppressing them all the time without any valid reasons. Therefore it is necessary to have an environment or an opportunity which would allow the participation of women. It includes raising awareness about rights - legal literacy, rights to education, and health. A systematic effort is needed to enhance women's understanding and awareness about various social and ethical issues.

Educating women is the most powerful instrument of changing their position at home, church and society. Education brings awareness, modification of behavior to adapt to situations, reduction in inequalities and also acts as a means to improve their status within the family. The empowerment of women implies building the capacity of women for restoring women's control over their own lives rather than being always dependent on others. Non-formal education through short term training programmes, conferences, seminars, adult education and literacy programs are important tools for empowering women. Over the past few years, all over the world, efforts have been made to empower women through literacy, education, and training at different levels. This can be achieved through mass media education, cell groups, seminars, meetings, pulpit teachings, Bible study, and women's self-help groups.

Clergy must give assistance to victims and perpetrators of abuse of women. He can become a helpful aid through proper theological education or training from senior clergy, by attending seminars and retreats or through proper understanding and observation of the nature and seriousness of abuse of women in Christian families. Clergy devote their lives to help the needy and to develop the God-given potential in the lives of members of their congregations. The constant touch with the issue or supervision or counseling will help clergymen to minimize abuse of women and to avoid entering into unhealthy or dangerous discussion or advice to victims. The clergy must recognize always that the Holy Spirit is the best counselor. Allow the Holy Spirit to guide and lead you throughout the process. The responsibility of Clergy is to help the victim as early as possible in an amicable way for the Glory of God with the help of senior clergy, legal experts, counselors and other NGO's. Clergyman cannot ignore this issue.

Many passages in the Bible articulate on the issue of abuse of women, and God's attitude toward those who repeatedly use violence. King David in Psalms 11:5 says "The LORD examines the righteous, but the wicked and those who love violence his soul hates." Again David in Psalms 37:9, "For evil men will be cut off, but those who hope in the LORD will inherit the earth." Malachi 2:16-17, "I hate divorce' says the LORD God of Israel, and I hate a man's covering himself with violence as well as with his garment," says the LORD Almighty....You have wearied the LORD with your words. "How have we wearied him?" you ask. By saying "all who do evil are good in the eyes of the LORD, and he is pleased with them," or "Where is the God of justice?" There are many such passages in the Bible.

Through his preaching, clergy can encourage the victims and lay a foundation for the members of the congregation to extend a helping hand to the victim and create an atmosphere for inner and outer healing. It is an opportunity of empowering and encouraging for abuse survivors to hear directly from the clergy. The members of the congregation need a series of teachings from the pulpit regarding abuse; signs, reasons, characteristics and nature of abuse and what the Bible teaches about the equality and dignity of women.

While helping the victim, clergy must recognize their own limitations and see clearly the complexities of abuse of women. Abuse of women is a complex issue; therefore it requires immediate attention and a solution has to be found as early as possible. Abuse of women or abuse of anybody results in deep seated inner wounds. The dynamics of abuse is complex and secret. For an outsider to know the exact truth is very difficult. Getting correct information from friends and relatives will be better than the clergy alone getting involved. Therefore, working with the abusive individual or her family calls for a partnership with the clergy or few spiritually oriented individuals from the congregation or likeminded agencies and professionals.

Clergy should take the initiative in teaching, preaching and empowering. He can organize or conduct workshops or seminars on a regular basis. Clergy must teach or preach about domestic abuse in sermons, Bible studies, and prayer meetings. In a nutshell, people must be made aware not in a philosophical manner, but through spiritual truth, in a practical and convincing manner. They should talk and discuss about building the family, practicing equality at home and to consider girls and boys equally. Partiality or favoritism to children should not be shown at any time.

The clergy and members of the church committee should encourage and ensure the participation of women in different sectors. They should not ignore or put down the talents and gifts which God has given to women in their congregation. Utilize their abilities and the opportunities available. Accept and appreciate their contribution and offer suggestions to lift the status of the women from their present state.

Jesus set an example for the empowerment of women during is public ministry. As followers of Christ, the members of the church and the clergymen should follow the example of Jesus Christ. In the Old Testament period women always had a second position compared to men. Jesus lifted the status of women to a position of equal worth and value with men, by admitting them to his inner circle of companions, and commissioning them to witness for him (Matt 12:49-50; 28:7; John 4:26-30; 20:17-18). Jesus' encounter with the Canaanite woman is an example of his appreciation of women (Matthew 15:21-28).This pagan woman had received recognition from Jesus. Jesus appreciated her faith, and granted a reward for her 'great faith.' (v28). Another encounter of Jesus with women was his appreciation for their faith and love (Luke 7:36-50). All four gospels have an account of 'a woman anointing Jesus'. He defends her action, even though many questions are raised including his disciple Judas Iscariot saying its waste of money. Jesus permitted her action. One can see Jesus' interaction in the case of the Samarian woman (John 4:1-15).

Apostle Paul speaks of women as 'fellow workers' (Romans 16:1-3, 6, 12; Philippians 4:2-3), persons who "have labored side by side with me in the gospel" (Philippians 4:3). Paul introduces them as 'our sisters' in Romans 16:1. This portrays a sense of belonging among fellow believers. They are an essential part of his ministry. In Philippians 4:2-3, these women associated with Paul for the sake of the gospel. Men and women are his equals and not subordinates (of.2:25; Romans 16:3, 9, 21).

Abuse of women is a reality of a very complex nature, inhuman behavior, destructive force, and not very easy to solve due to the inner wounds rather than physical one. Clergy have a great role and utilize the necessary influence to bring a healing touch and arrange protection for the abused families. Develop a ministry among the victims and even among the perpetrators. Then severity of the abuse reduces day by day, so that the congregation is a safe, secure and a healing place for abusive families and abusive members. Through this God's name may be honored and glorified.

According to Kamala Bhasin, 'Empowerment of women' means, "recognizing women's contribution and women's knowledge. It means helping women fight their own fears, and feelings of inadequacy and inferiority. It means women enhance their self respect and self dignity. It means women controlling their own bodies. It means women becoming economically independent and self reliant. It means women controlling resources like land and property. It means reducing women's burden of work, especially within the home. It means creating and strengthening women's groups and organizations. It means promoting qualities of nurturing, caring, gentleness, not just in women but also in men."[13]

"Empowerment of women would necessarily mean redefining the notions of feminity and masculinity changing man-woman relationship. ... We want men who are gentle, who are caring .The models of good men for us are not muscular, aggressive, supermen but men like Jesus Christ. We want husbands who can not only act as fathers but also as mothers."[14]

There are many instances where women play an important role in God's plan in both Testaments. Miriam, the prophetess, focused her ministry on the women of Israel (Exodus 15:20). Deborah, another prophetess, became a national judge of Israel (Judges 4:4; 5:7). Isaiah's wife (Isaiah 8:3), Huldah, another prophetess, was consulted by Josiah's chief men for her opinion (2 Kings 22:14-20). Noadiah (Nehemiah 6:14) Jael, a noted woman of respect, was a living indictment to the weakness of Barak and other men in Israel (Judges 4:9); and it was Abigail (1 Samuel 25), who, persuaded David not to kill her husband Nabal. Anna (Luke 2:36), praised God for the child Jesus and Philip's daughters (Acts 21:9)These four daughters were dedicated in a special way to serve the Lord (of 1 Cor. 7:34).

15

At Jacob's well near Sychar, Jesus talked with a Samaritan woman, telling her that he was the Messiah, the Son of God. John 4:4-42.

All the four gospels represent Jesus as the one who fully accepted women in his public ministry without any hesitation or reservations. He talked to them, had fellowship with them and healed them, regardless of sex, social or marital barriers, His unfailingly well-mannered, and compassionate attitude towards them was appreciable. When a woman, ritually unclean with a hemorrhage, touched Him on the way to the house of a synagogue leader, He stopped His journey and healed her and admired her faith so much, addressing her affectionately as 'Daughter' (Mark 5:34). He declared the dignity of a crippled woman, calling her a 'daughter of Abraham' (Luke 13:16). Jesus healed Peter's mother-in-law (Mark 1:29-31), as well as Jairus's daughter (5:35-43), Mary Magdalene and the Syro-Phoenician woman's daughter (even though she was a Gentile); and restored to life the son of the widow at Nain (Luke 7:11-15).

Apostle Paul

Aquila and Priscilla are mentioned by Paul. He counts this couple as his fellow workers (Romans 16:3-5). They were obviously a husband-wife evangelical team. In Romans 16, thought to be a list of Ephesian Christians, in addition to Priscilla and Aquila, there are 24 personal names. Of these five are feminine, and two unnamed women also appear. Paul does not differentiate between services rendered by men and women. Apostle Paul to Galatians 3:28, "There is neither Jew nor Greek, slave nor free, male nor female, for you are all one in Christ Jesus." Here Apostle Paul overthrows ethical, social and gender distinction. He is not against any gender as some people believe.

Jawaharlal Nehru, the first Prime Minister of India once said, "You can tell the condition of a nation by looking at the status of its women."[16] Women of any nation are the mirror of its civilization. This is very much true in this present context. Jesus gives a clear cut teaching about the status and dignity of women. That is an example to each one of us. "Woman is the companion of man, gifted with equal mental capacities. She has the right to participate in very minute detail in the activities of man and she has an equal right of freedom and liberty with him."[17]

A strong question could arise whether one could tell the condition of the church by looking at the status of women! A church which discriminates against one sex cannot be effective. A healthy church should make use of the gifts and talents of every human being, whether of male or female, for is glory and the extension of is kingdom.

Endnotes

[1] Webster's seventh new collegiate Dictionary, (Springfield: G. & C. Merriam Co. Publishers, 1971), "Teach", 905.

[2] Wesley Carr (ed), *The New Dictionary of Pastoral Studies* (Michigan: Eerdmans Publishing Co., 2002), "Care", 43.

[3] Carr (ed), *The New Dictionary of Pastoral Studies*, 76.

[4] Bruce Perry, "The Neuro- developmental Impact of Violence in Childhood," in Textbook of Child and Adolescent Forensic Psychiatry, eds. D. Schetky and E. Benedek (Washington, D.C.: American Psychiatric Press, 2001), 21-38.

[5] Personal Observations. (Kottayam, 15 July 2005).

[6] Personal Conversation, (Thiruvalla, 20 June 2007).

[7] Sr. Dr. Joan Chunkapura and Ms. Celine Manayani, *Women for women* (Bangalore: Sunshine Publications, 2006), 65.

[8] *Capacities Building for Empowerment. Report of a Workshop held in Jinja. Uganda. 6-8 March 2005.* Unpublished report for Oxfam GB. 2005, 7.

[9] *http://www.rrtd.nic.in/international%20women.htm.   http://www.wed.nic.in/empowerment.htm. (accessed 18 June 2006).*

[10] Sandra Morgen &Ann Bookman, "Rethinking women and politics: an introductory essay," *Women and Politics of empowerment* (Philadelphia: Temple University Press, 1988), 3-32.

[11] Beula Ruth W, *Protect yourself* (Secunderabad: OM Headlines, 2004), 59.

[12] *http://revlady.hubpages.com/hub/Status-of-Women-in-Old-and-New-Testaments.* Follow us @E Journal_USA twitter.com/ EJournal_USA-The official voice of United States society, culture and values. *(accessed 20 August 2007).*

[13] Kamala Bhasin, "Education for women's empowerment: Some reflections" *Adult Education And Development*, No:39, March, 1992, 19-20. She is developing strategies for participatory development, popular education, women's empowerment.

[14] Bhasin, "Education for women," 20.

[15] *http://revlady.hubpages.com/hub/Status-of-Women-in-Old-and-New-Testaments.* Follow us @ E Journal, USA twitter.com/ E Journal_USA-The official voice of United States society, culture and values. *(accessed 25 July 2006).*

[16] Carol S.Coonrod, "Chronic Hunger and the Status of Women in India," *The Hunger Project.* June (1998). "Millennium Development Goals." *http://www.developmentgoals.org/Hiv_Aids.htm#target 7* (accessed 10 October 2009). Gargi D. Khare, "Millennium Development Goals: A Focus on HIV/AIDS in Indian Women," *MURJ Journal* Volume 11 (2004), 27.

[17] _____ *M K Gandhi, 1933.*

Chapter 5

Analysis of Data

T he respondents shared information which is given along with charts and tables. The respondents were assured that their identity would not be revealed and all the information collected would be dealt with in strict confidence. The women willingly took time off their daily routine and shared their life experiences with our data collectors. There were women who wanted to talk but could not because of the watching eyes of family members. Some dared to take the risk and poured out bottled up feelings and sufferings. A few others asked to reschedule the interviews according to their time and place when they could talk fearlessly and freely. These additional anecdotal notes received by data collectors contain practical informations and are very useful.

Analysis of Responses from Married Christian Women

As the research topic is a sensitive issue, the respondents were selected by using the following criteria set by the researcher. The respondents were married Indian Christian women, who were willing to co-operate with the study, were reliable, and willing to share or discuss the issue of abuse. These women were selected from different denominations with the help of clergy, evangelists, nuns, Christian women workers, friends and relatives.

The author would like to explain here that the selection of respondents was possibly weighed in favour of finding women who could speak on the subject of abuse, since those selected may have been chosen by informants for this reason.

The same questions were used for questionnaires and interviews. Questions were prepared in English. The data collectors translated these into the respondents' own language when and where need arises.

These women from different denominations namely the Church of South India, Church of North India, St. Thomas Evangelical Church of India, Catholic Church, Syrian Marthoma, Brethren Church, Pentecostal Church, Syrian Orthodox, and Methodist Church. The study was restricted to abuse of women by their husbands in Indian Christian families.

TABLE 1
Respondents (Women) and their Denomination

Denomination	No
Church of South India	10
Church of North India	15
St. Thomas Evangelical Church of India (STECI)	15
Catholic Church	08
Syrian Marthoma Church	12
Brethren Church	10
Pentecostal Church	15
Syrian Orthodox Church	10
Methodist Church	05
Total	100

Marriage Duration
The majority of the respondents (56 %) had been married between 0-10 years.

CHART 1
Marriage Duration

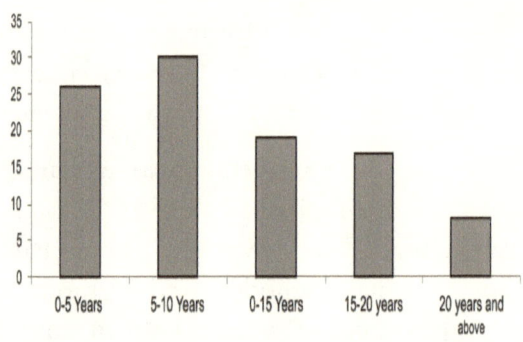

Educational Qualifications of Husband and Wife

The educational qualifications of the husband and wife are grouped as under- graduates, graduates, and post-graduates. Under-graduates included those who have studied from first standard to twelfth standard. It is estimated from the respondents, that when there was disparity in the educational background of husband and wife, the abuse of women took place, especially when the wife was more educationally qualified than the husband.

CHART 2
Educational Qualifications of the Husbands and Wife

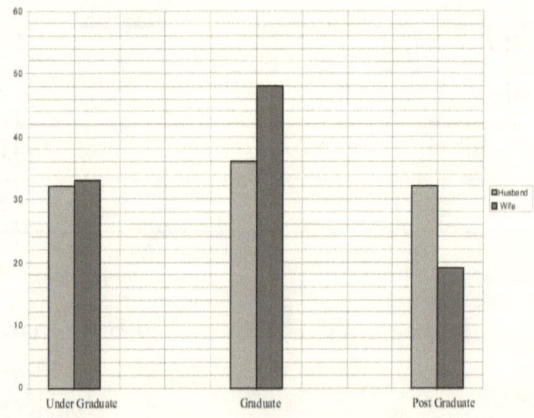

Women: Employed and Non-employed

Out of the one hundred respondents, sixty-nine percent of the women were employed and thirty-one percent were home makers. Women who were employed were working as IT professionals, engineers, teachers, doctors, nurses, journalists, bank employees, housemaids, and coolie workers. Doctors and nurses had to be on night duty often. A few women working in the IT sector, especially those working in call centers shared that the working time for husband and wife are dissimilar. One of the journalists had unscheduled lengthy working hours. The housemaids were engaged for twenty-four hours if it was necessary to stay at the house where they were working. This points to the possibility that employed women and men find it hard to maintain work-life balance especially if the husband is not co-operative in taking equal share in the responsibilities of the home. The situation becomes worse if they get different or unscheduled working hours. Then the burden and stress will be more.

Most of the employed women had to take care of the entire household tasks after returning from the work place. This will affect her physical and mental health; social life is also hindered due to insufficient time.

Some of the employed women shared that though they are regularly earning, they have no control over their finances. Financial dependence on husbands by the non-employed women is greater when compared to their employed counterparts. They need to completely depend on their husbands for every minute thing. A few non- employed home makers said that they did not have any assistance from the husband at home and are expected to complete the entire household work, shopping, taking care of the children and if there is an elderly person at home, to care for them as well.

CHART 3
Employment Status

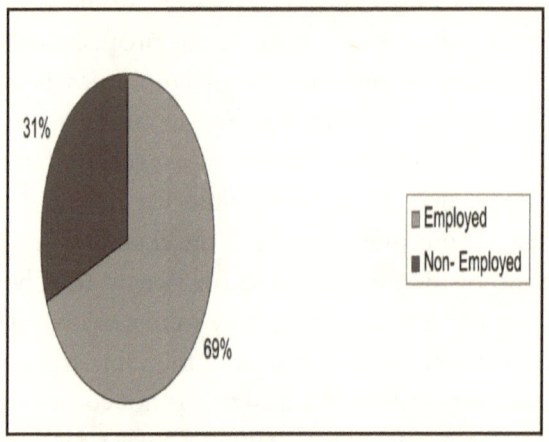

CHART 4
Employment Status of Urban
and Rural Respondents -Comparison

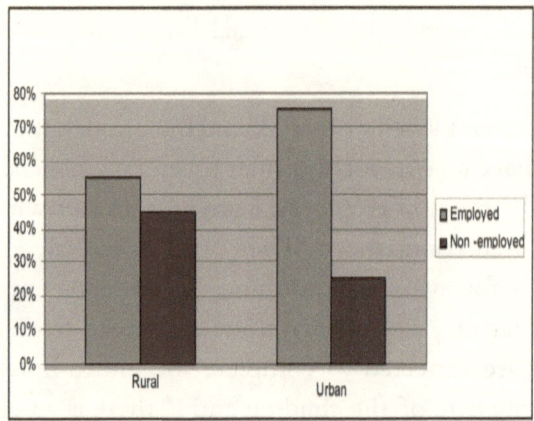

In both rural and urban areas, the percentage of employed women is found to be more when compared to their non-employed counterparts. A few urban women said that they are financially independent because of their employment. Even though the employed women seem to be financially independent, a few shared that they experienced occasional financial abuse from husbands, in-laws and other relatives. A few women, who are at present residing in urban areas, said that earlier they were in rural areas and moved to cities after their marriage. Employment opportunities for women are more in urban areas than in the rural region. In rural areas it is understood from non-employed women that financial stress and strain was one of the major causes of abuse.

A few husbands are alcoholics with no regular jobs. When there was no money for drinks, wife-beating started along with verbal abuse. In some cases the abuse became very severe and the victims and their children were forced to take shelter away from the husbands for protection.

Experience of Abuse in Marital Life

The term, 'abuse' includes to hurt, ill-treat, injure, insult, to use coarse language, deceitful acts and being unfair to the other person. When the term abuse comes to mind, it is often thought of as physical abuse as it is publicized more by the media. Physical abuse causes external injuries such as bruises, cuts and fractures which leave visible marks on the body. If the physical abuse is severe, it can be a threat to life. Physical abuse is the one which is always easily noticeable by others. Medical attention is sought or given in most of the cases. This is probably one of the reasons why others come to know about it or the media highlights it more as physical abuse. They are less focused on the other forms of abuse. In other words the harshness of physical abuse or its rate of recurrence is given more weight when abuse is talked about.

The outward appearance of abuse is interrelated and interconnected. It is a shocking revelation that ninety-two percentage of the respondents shared that they have experienced some form of abuse from their husbands in their marital life either quite regularly or once in a while. However the researcher would like to explain the reasons for this high percentage. The majority of the respondents said that the most common form of abuse is psychological abuse which leaves a permanent and deep seated scar in their minds. Psychological abuse is a more intense form of abuse. Nobody can easily recognize the psychological abuse that a woman suffers, when compared to other forms of abuses. It is unexplainable and most often it is not shared with, or identified by, others. The impact of psychological abuse can be apparent in various ways affecting their physical, emotional, social and spiritual health. This may lead to physical illnesses like peptic ulcer, heart disease, or bronchial asthma. It even affects the new born baby if the abused mother is breast feeding or pregnant. Psychological abuse can lead to social withdrawal of the abuser. Some of the diseases, confusions and disorders disturbing the mind include depression, anxiety and insomnia. All these prove beyond doubt, how psychological abuse affects the women as well as the children young or old and other members of the family.

Therefore clergy should be aware of the importance of psychological stress the women endure during or after the abuse. This fact should be kept in mind by the clergy while preaching, teaching and counseling.

Eight percent of the married women said that they did not suffer any form of abuse from their husbands. It appears they are saying their husbands are extremely perfect spouse. The author recognizes the possibility that these women were not willing or comfortable to talk about the issue of abuse due to some sort of embarrassment, control of some form and suspicion, or they may feel that any abuse they are facing is negligible. One of the respondents even claimed that fights between the spouses and the compromising after it is common in Christian families, and that this increases the affection and creates better understanding between the spouses. This is a common response by the eight percent of the married women. The interpretation of this statement will depend on the meaning of the word 'fight'. If it does not go beyond a limit and there is full control of the situation, it is alright. Most of the time it goes beyond our control due to the interference of Satan.

The author did not intend to find the severity or frequency of abuse of women. The purpose of this study was not to show a percentage of women who have experienced abuse in their married life; but rather its implications for the family and the church. The researcher's aim is to confirm that abuse is real and prevalent even today. Therefore we need to find a solution for this unbiblical, unethical and unpleasant occurrence in families and in the Church. We cannot ignore this fact. Therefore, we need to find a remedy for it and try to build strong and healthy families. For this, the church and clergy play an essential role. They must work together for a unique cause.

CHART 5
Forms of Abuse-Rural and Urban

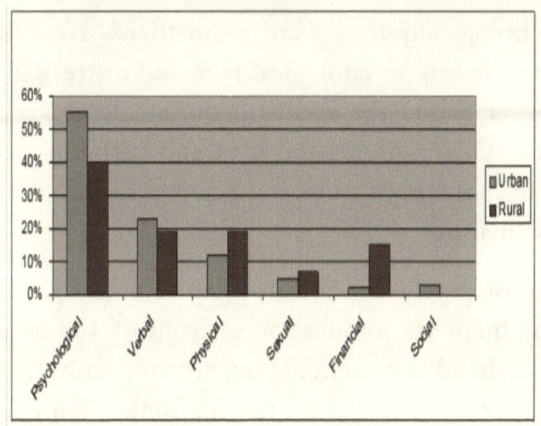

Forms of Abuse- Rural and Urban

The author developed a number of simple definitions for the different forms of abuse (verbal, physical, psychological, sexual, financial and social) as it became an essential requirement for uniformity in the data collection. It is obvious that the respondents may not have been able to keep the same dimensions or meaning which the author had intended. Therefore some simple meanings and definitions were given to the interviewers as well as to the respondents. Abuse of women is a deliberate behavior. The purpose of abuse is to establish and exercise power and control over a weaker person.

Psychological Abuse

Psychological abuse is very complex and is difficult to capture in a study like this. It has been found that severe psychological stress and living under the cloud of terror and the mental torture of abuse can lead to self-destructive behavior and to consequences like suicide.

It is learned that psychological, verbal and social abuse is more common for urban married women. Physical, sexual, psychological and financial abuse is on the higher side for rural women compared to urban women. This may be due to the lower educational level, substance abuse of husbands and low socio-economic background.

When the respondents were asked about the diverse forms of abuse experienced, they revealed that the physical pain was temporary whereas psychologically they were traumatized. Nevertheless every abuse ultimately led to psychological pain and distress. They said that they could never forget the incident; the incidents keep on ringing in their minds. This indicates the hurt and suffering of the abused women who have the right to be respected, recognized and treated in a fair and just manner.

The forms of psychological abuse experienced by married women as narrated by them are humiliation in front of the family members or in public; husband not spending quality time with the wife; lack of transparency; spending most of the time in front of the TV, computer or newspaper or with friends, isolating the wife from all family discussion and decision making; and doubts about her fidelity. These create an atmosphere of fear of isolation. This is apart from the description in the definition in chapter one. Moreover, ninety-two percent of women who experienced psychological abuse were exposed to more than one form of abuse. When the abuse recurs and is ongoing, it makes the abuse all the more serious.

In addition to instant physical injury, violence can lead women to a number of immediate and long term effects such as infectious diseases, mental health problems, injuries, chronic pain syndrome, gastrointestinal problems, hypertension, and asthma.

The following details were obtained from the discussion between the interviewer and the person interviewed. It was seen that, if the wife was abroad, she suffered more psychological as well as financial abuse from the husband. In one of the cases the wife was forced to go abroad leaving her small children. She was asked to send all her earnings from there and most of the time this was spent lavishly by the in-laws rather than saving it for their family. They never acknowledged that it was her hard labour that enabled them to spend extravagantly.

If the husband was abroad, then also the psychological abuse of women was higher. One of the respondents shared that her husband was working abroad. As he was away, she had to shoulder every aspect of the family responsibilities- taking care of children and in-laws; if the in-laws are bedridden then the situation is much worse, purchasing provisions for home, paying bills, meeting the medical needs and more socialization. She has to do all these things if the children are small. He grew suspicious when she was not found at home when he telephoned her from abroad. In addition to this, the in-laws started to exert more control over her. He could not understand the various family responsibilities as she was managing everything single handedly.

Five women shared that their husband's illnesses were not mentioned to their parents when the alliance was finalized. Out of the five, two of them had mental illness, one had renal transplant, one had juvenile diabetes and the fifth with heart disease. Being loyal and loving wives they had decided to stick to the marriage though their psychological, social or biological needs were not met as they desired. Dependent husbands are a cause of great concern.

Verbal Abuse

One respondent revealed that she was verbally abused by her husband every day after consuming alcohol, or when he gets irritated or angry. He abuses her loudly with filthy and cursing words. She is humiliated in front of children, neighbors and family members. An employed respondent in a managerial position said that her husband used sarcastic and abusive words even while telephoning her at the office. He often visited her in the office and talked in the same manner in front of the junior colleagues and senior officers. Therefore he did not treat her like a life partner. This led her to mental depression and humiliation.

This was the routine behavior of her husband. He professed to be a born-again Christian, and was also an active leader in his church. What a pathetic situation!

Physical Abuse

With tearful eyes the women showed scars on their bodies as a result of the beating, burning, pushing, throwing objects, pulling hair, and kicking. This was always accompanied by verbal and psychological abuse. Women are neglected and discriminated against with regard to food and medical facilities. This kind of behavior invites sickness and soon death.

One husband hailing from a Christian family was involved with occult activities. He believed in sorcery and forced his wife to do the same. Their family was under great financial stress and he strongly believed that she was the cause for this. He regularly practiced 'black magic' and 'calling the spirits of the dead'. The wife, a true believer, could not tolerate this. She was physically and psychologically abused in many ways. He attempted to kill her and the children.

Sexual Abuse

One of the married women who was born and brought up in a good Christian family was forced by her husband to watch and read pornographic materials and act accordingly. According to her belief, this is a sin. However she was forced into it and to perform perverted or deviated sex. When she refused she was physically forced by her abuser.

Seven women said that they did not have the right to refuse sex when their husbands demanded or forced it upon them, even when they were not in mood for sex because they were tired, ill or upset. Regularly there will be arguments or fights which create an unpleasant atmosphere. The wives said that after all this they really did not want to engage in any sexual activities. Despite this their husbands forced them. If they did not allow their husbands to engage in the activities, again there would be a bad scene.

Financial Abuse

Two women were married into very affluent families. These women are beautiful, talented, well-educated and hailed from middle class families. The dowry was waived off as their husbands were less educated and the women were expected to take care of the ailing parents- in-law. These women are compelled to remain at home taking care of the sick and performing all the household chores. In certain cases the husbands boasted in front of his friends and relatives that they sacrificed greatly in marrying women from a lower economic background, causing embarrassment and humiliation to the wife. They remained in the marriage as they did not want to upset their parents or bring shame to their families.

One lady shared that hers was an 'exchange marriage'. (Example: Mr. X is married to Mr. Y's daughter. Mr. Y's son is given in marriage to Mr. X's sister) She was forced to marry a mentally challenged person. This was primarily because her family could not afford to pay the amount demanded as dowry. She was forced into marriage so that her sisters could have better alliances. Her husband's family promised to pay the dowry and meet the other expenses for the sister's wedding.

A few women said that they are never included while decisions are made on purchasing land or major investments etc. though they feel that they are capable of deciding on these matters along with their husbands.

Social Abuse

Social abuse is a less prominent form of domestic violence than we think. One woman shared that her husband has some bad habits which she did not appreciate. She shared her concerns and told him to change the habits like talking loudly while eating, gluttony, screaming for everything, and not replacing things. The husband continued doing it purposefully to take vengeance on her. It was always embarrassing to go out for parties or to socialize along with her husband.

Eight women said that they have restricted freedom of movement outside the house without their husband or in-laws permission or their presence. They were not permitted to go alone to the market place, to a place of worship, to the hospital, or even to visit parents, friends and relatives without being escorted by their husbands or husband's agents. Coercion of an individual in a social surrounding; joint abuse by a group of people toward one individual; barring social contact with others for various activities; controlling what the victim does and whom she sees, not giving the victim any time alone, and controlling what the victim wears are all forms of Social Abuse. However their husband did not have any time to escort them and thus these privileges were often denied. Embarrassment, intimidation, and emotional abuse may all be forms of social abuse. They are always under the control or the restriction of husband or in- laws. They don't even have the freedom to move around freely in a relaxed manner.

All the above incidents narrate the different forms of abuse experienced by married women in so called Christian families. After reading these one may come to the conclusion that this is not at all true in Christian families and that such practices do not happen in Christian families, or that this is an exaggeration. Others may say this is the first time they are hearing of such incidents in Christian families and they are not aware of this. People will have mixed feelings about the incidents. Some may say we are different than non-Christian families. Yes we need to be different. But most of the time we are not different from others. Sometimes we are worse than non-Christians.

CHART 6
Marital Duration at which Spousal Abuse First Occured

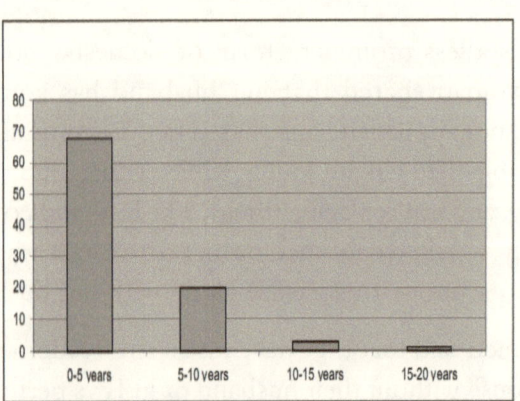

The majority of the women experienced abuse for the first time during the first five years of marriage. This is almost similar to that of National Family Health Survey (NFHS-3) Domestic Violence, 2005-2006) which is given in chapter 2.

The conversations during data collection revealed that the majority of the marriages were arranged by parents, friends, relatives, agents or matrimony.com. Most of the husbands did not know much about their wives, nor the wives about their husbands before the marriage, due to the system of arranged marriage. A few admitted that they did not have any time together to get to know each other. They both had great expectations about each other which were not communicated in a realistic and meaningful manner. It is a South Indian practice that the newly married couples visit all the close relatives, friends and elders after the marriage. Usually the very next day the visits begin. Friends and relatives invite them for breakfast, lunch or dinner parties. This goes on for few days. Traveling to different places was very tedious. Once it is time for couples to be back to their respective work, they realize that they did not have any quality quiet time together as most of their time was spent in the presence of others through talking, visiting or in traveling.

In the urban set up, working schedules may be different; because of the shift system the husband and wife are rarely together at home, having very little time together. At times open communication is very limited to 'matter-of–fact' conversations. They usually have telephonic conversation. With the work pressure at the office and home, a small problem can ignite or perceived as a major problem, and this finally leads to harassment or abuse of women. Abuse can be prevented if we follow one basic principle, 'Never major on minor things'. Most abuse is due to majoring on minor things. If the husband or wife is out of station in connection with their work, the separation away from the spouse causes tension, anxiety, stress, strain, or doubts which may lead to psychological abuse.

CHART 7
Reasons for Abuse

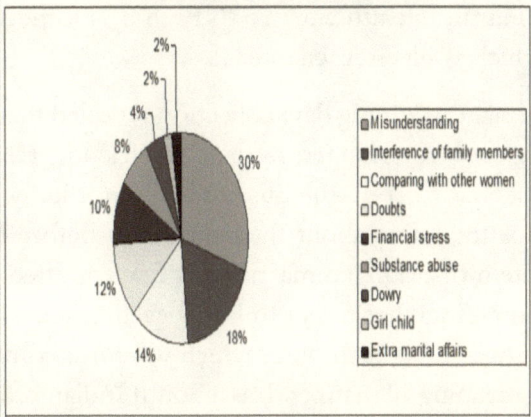

- Misunderstanding
- Interference of family members
- Comparing with other women
- Doubts
- Financial stress
- Substance abuse
- Dowry
- Girl child
- Extra marital affairs

Misunderstandings

Thirty percent of the married women said that the main reason for abuse was misunderstanding between the spouses. The misunderstanding was due to many reasons. Misunderstanding is caused through ego clashes (inferiority, superiority complex), disparity in education, employment and family status, involvement of the in-laws, differentiation in thinking and personality. A few said that husbands were resentful and angry of their wives' achievements and were jealous of any one praising them. A few men or in-laws were trying to get private information about their wives or were listening to gossip. This caused misunderstanding and later led to doubts or suspicions. They never took time to enquire or listen to the wife's explanations.

For some, her involvement in social or church related activities is not appreciated. Many women who are educated and want to study further are not allowed to do so because of the fear that she may surpass her husband. These are all due to an inferiority complex.

Interference of the Family Members

The husbands want to justify the act of abusing their wives. The married women were asked to give the reasons for abuse by their husbands. They responded that interference of the family members, especially in-laws comparing them with other women, or having doubts were the factors of misunderstanding. Eighteen percent said that usually their husbands are provoked by the in-laws to demand more money or other possession; if they are unwilling to do this, abuse starts. The in-laws try to control and manipulate the family life of the couple. The husband may not understand the wife.

Unnecessary interference of family members was a strong point brought out by several women who were abused. Usually in-laws convince or persuade their son to bring extra money and household articles in addition to the demanded dowry. The in-laws, having a great influence over the son, demand his full attention, money and time. In many families they are in full control of the son's finances. In some families the mother or father or both of them give guidance on what to do and what not to do. The son is still under their influence and guidance. He does not have freedom to take independent decisions. Bringing up the children, religious rituals, education and decisions on higher education of the children, choosing professions for the children, construction of house, and place of settlement are often decided by the senior male in the patriarchal family. Many women said that they are capable, competent and confident in managing the family whereas the husband is afraid to allow them to do so.

Discrepancy between the spouses occurs especially with regard to child rearing practices. The in-laws also interfere in this regard. The husband and in-laws compare the wife with other women whose children are well behaved and she is blamed for their rebellious attitude. The husband and in-laws are well aware that she is a working woman, and time is limited for her to look after the children. Therefore both husband and wife are to share and shoulder the responsibility to raise the children according to Biblical ways, it is not the task of the woman or mother alone. Raising children is a two way system. This incongruity between husband and wife is a leading cause of abuse in the family.

Comparison with other Women

Often women are compared with other women, to be more precise, with mother, sister, friend's wife, and celebrities. He expresses that the other women are smarter, more beautiful and more efficient than her. These comments make her psychologically depressed. She feels that she is worthless or insignificant. The in-laws and her husband must know that every woman is unique in the sight of God. Comparison is not a problem solver; it is an inventor of problems. Accepting her as she is, is the best medicine for the cure of abuse of woman. Unrealistic or impractical expectations of husbands about their wives are the main reason for ill-treatment. Day after-day this ill-treatment continuous, leading to harassment and abuse. The researcher feels that all these can be prevented if the husband and wife spend some time to understand each other and recognize their strengths, weakness, interests, pattern of life system, and their priorities in life.

A woman was married to a divorcee. The couple was happy in the beginning. Later he started to compare her with his previous wife, her culinary expertise and beauty. His criticism always belittled her. This is a severe psychological abuse and still continues. Never compare your spouse with others. She is a unique person with a unique personality. Acknowledge her as a God given partner for you. That will make a lot of difference in dealing with her.

Doubts

There can be healthy and unhealthy doubts. Some doubts are normal, and have a favorable impact while others are abnormal and have a destructive impact on relationships, especially marital relationships. Unhealthy doubts need to be controlled in the beginning itself, so that they does not spread like wild fire. A small doubt can grow to a bigger one, and cannot be relinquished very easily.

Doubts by husbands also play a key role in abuse of wives. These doubts may even lead the husband to strong suspicion, especially if he suspects that his wife is having an extra marital affair. There are people known to the researcher who even trace the phone calls of their wives. Without clarifying the doubts from the wife directly, they degrade her by abusing her. A few women said that their husbands doubted their chastity. Many working women faced abuse as the husbands doubted their relationships with male colleagues in the work area. One respondent said that disparity in education influenced her husband to abuse her as she was more qualified than her husband. Husbands also enjoyed using their muscle power to dominate.

Financial Stress

Seventeen women said that they are unaware of the finances in their own family. Some working women are expected to give their entire salary to the husbands. He is to be requested each time for money, even for local travel expenses. Some husbands are spendthrifts yet four of them were engaged in gambling. Some were giving loans to friends; eating out and entertaining friends in eateries, thus spending a lot of money. Some husbands spend a lot of income without taking into consideration their family. Finally they end up in financial crisis. Some people do not have a family budget. The wife and children do not have enough money to meet the necessities of life. If the husband was confronted, it ended in abuse. Many of these men never believed in giving tithes. They had never learned at their home regarding giving to God's work. For this reason tithe was considered to be an expense item. Knowing how to manage the family finances is a great way to solve the abuse of women in families.

A married woman said that hers was a love marriage. Their parents were strongly opposed to the marriage. When they had financial problems, the husband forced her to approach her parents. She neither had support from her parents nor from the husband. She was in a great dilemma and agony.

Greed or excessive desire to have 'things' led a couple to be childless. Instead of having treatment for sterility, the husband sent his wife abroad to earn extra money. He advised her to encash all her leave so that she could send more money. Her health deteriorated as she continued doing extra hours of work. Time could not wait and later she had secondary sterility. She had to discontinue her job because of ill-health. She regrets not having treatment at the right time. Her husband and his family blame her for not giving birth to any children.

Dowry

Another important factor that results in the abuse of women in families is the matter of dowry. The media reports daily about dowry deaths, suicides of the entire family including children, as a result of financial issues. Demanding more dowries after the marriage and failure to meet the demands set by the husband and family before the marriage creates problems. Moreover financial stress or crisis can occur as a result of substance abuse and gambling by the husbands. As a result the husband demands that the wife brings more money or dowry from her home and if not, he starts abusing her physically and mentally.

Girl Child

Having girl children is also an excuse for some to abuse their wives. They think that it is due to the fault of the wife that a girl child is born. As society encourages dowry, the birth of a girl child is often not a happy moment. It is sad to see that women have to suffer abuse from their husbands for this. Even though they are not at fault some husbands abuse their wives because of this.

Extra Marital Affairs

Two women said that their husbands had extra marital affairs and were abused when they questioned it. Husbands have to be faithful to their own wives.

Though some of what is narrated here are incidents that occurred to only one or a few married women, considering the immeasurable amount of abuse women undergo, the researcher decided to bring these incidents to light.

Often the wife is blamed for the children being rebellious and disobedient and the father tends to be authoritarian. Both husband and wife do not have a common understanding or a united front when the children are disciplined.

Grieving for loved ones is common, but blaming the wife for the death of his parents or child will cause added psychological stress to the woman. In fact a child was diagnosed as having a brain tumor and the prognosis was explained to the family by the doctors. Instead of being sensitive and compassionate, one woman was shouted at by the husband at the time of the funeral for killing the child.

Mistakes in the work area or losing a job were placed on the woman's shoulders. Bitterness and resentment of the husband were held as another reason for abuse. The wife was unaware of the cause of his bitterness.

One woman expressed the view that men consider their wives to be 'shock absorbers' – a wife is a person specially created to bear all the accusations, blame, tension, anxiety, and worries without exhibiting any reaction.

Worshipping in separate churches because they belonged to two different denominations was another cause of abuse in three families. The husband insisted on the wife and children joining him in his place of worship. She did not believe in the fundamental doctrines of the church he was attending.

One woman said that the dictatorship of her husband and his controlling her in front of others is always humiliating. He enjoyed his supremacy and expected absolute submission from her. She suffered in silence as she was unable to react in public.

The research and the incidental reports show that abusers expect to have things their way and if they do not get it, they abuse their wives. This reflects the culture they are in.

The abuser is often raised in a culture where the wife is expected to be obedient, obliging, loving, forgiving the husband, not raising her voice against him. These beliefs have been molded in his mind from childhood. The influence of his family and neighborhood and his upbringing are some of the factors which make him believe that he has the right to abuse his wife.

Miscommunication can take place where a sender sends a message and the receiver misinterprets it, does not grasp it or understand the full details, or does not recognize what was the intention of the sender.

Miscommunication between the spouses aggravated abuse. However each time the wife was blamed for it.

Besides this, a woman is made to believe by society, by the family she grew up in, and by her spouse that she is the reason for the abuse, whereas it is an excuse of the husband to abuse his wife.

Place of Abuse

According to the study, fifty-three percent of the married women stated that abuse takes place usually behind closed doors, usually in the bedroom. There is no eye-witnesses for these incidents of abuse. Therefore, there is no real proof to confirm whether the abuse took place or not, or to what extent; when it took place; and how severe the abuse was. While the abuse took place behind closed doors most of the husbands ensured that the noise of crying or abusing was not heard outside the room. Thirty-two percent say that abuse was experienced in front of the immediate family which included the young or older children. The immediate family includes husband, wife and children. Eleven percent claimed that they had experienced abuse in front of the extended family. Extended families include husband, wife, children, his parents, and other in-laws. Four percent said that they were abused in front of outsiders or family members.

CHART 8
Place of Abuse

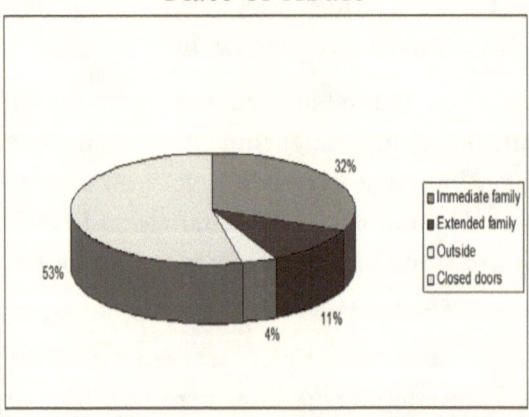

Initial Reaction to Abuse

It was distressing, painful, or upsetting to learn the initial reaction to abuse. 46% were in despair feeling helpless and lonely. An additional 40% were angry although they were not sure whom the anger was against. A further 09% went to the extent of attempting suicide, and 05% felt divorce was the only solution.

In a nutshell 95% of the women had feelings of helplessness which were manifested as anger (40%), utter despair (46%) and as thoughts of ending life (9%). In the initial stage the woman is shocked, not bold enough to share her problems even with her parents, siblings, friends or others. This is not a pleasant subject for discussion. Some people do not want to hear this topic, and others enjoy hearing the incidents for gossip. Therefore she keeps all the frustrations, feelings of guilt, shame, and humiliation within. As a result the helplessness is projected as anger to herself, the people close to her or even to God. These depressing thoughts lead to the suicidal tendency.

Due to the severity of abuse some felt that there is no one, not even God, to help them. Some even thought of committing suicide after suffering the abuse without thinking of its consequences. They attempted to end their life by hanging, cutting their veins, consuming poison, electrocution, jumping inside the well, jumping from multi-storied buildings or burning themselves with volatile substances like kerosene, cooking gas, or petrol. Some of them immediately thought about their children and parents and changed their mind. A few realized that suicide is not the solution for their problem.

They even questioned God for creating them to suffer like this. A very small percentage of women took a bold decision to live and provide a safe, secure and fear-free home for the children. One woman said that she will not give her husband legal separation, it will be a 'sweet revenge' but she will be living separately.

CHART 9
Initial Reaction to Abuse

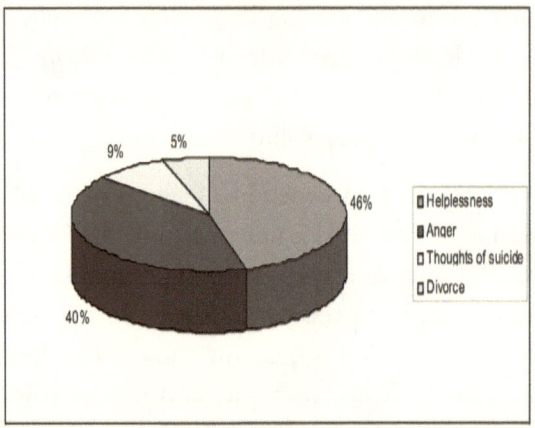

Chart 10 shows that the initial reaction of the majority (95%) of the married women was helplessness. Even though they were helpless in the initial stage, their social and spiritual affinities lead them to seek some kind of help; 64% women sought help.

CHART 10

Help Sought during Abuse

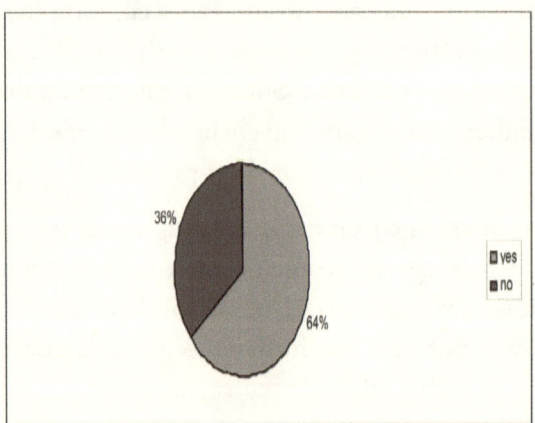

For the people who sought help, different varieties of help or advice was received. This is explained in chart 16.

CHART 11
Comparative Study -
Urban and Rural Married Women who Sought Help

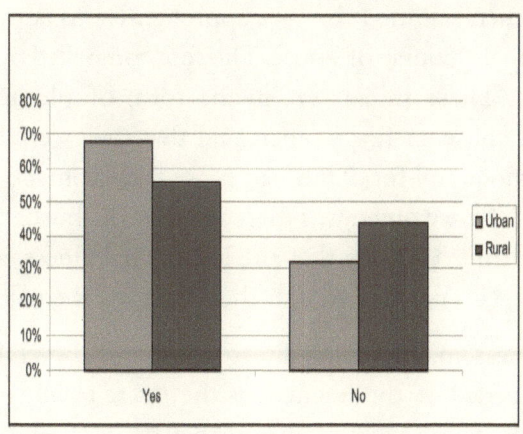

More of the urban women sought help during the course of abuse when compared with their rural counterparts. The urban women are educated, most of them were employed. Opportunities for seeking help are more for the urban women than rural. Most of the rural women are uneducated, unemployed and had less chance of professional help. Those who did not seek help said that they feared gossip, people knowing about this abuse, and disgrace.

CHART 12
Reasons for not Seeking Help

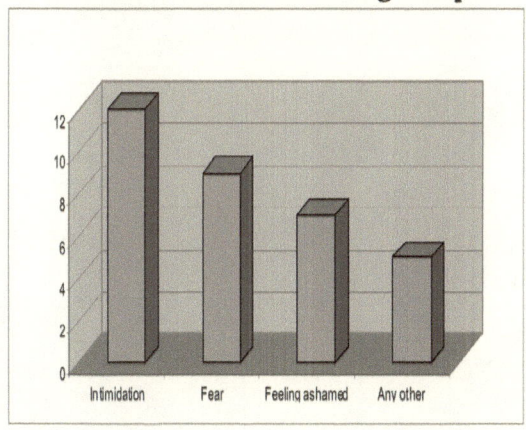

The following information regarding 'reasons for not seeking help' is collected through the questionnaires, personal interviews and observations.

Many women said that they are apprehensive to approach anyone for help during the course of abuse. They are compelled by intimidation to keep quiet. These threats are in the form of physical, verbal or psychological abuse. A few women said that they were locked inside the room without any food and had no outside contact. Two women were throttled. One woman was threatened by the husband saying that he would inform everybody that she has mental illness, and has extra marital affairs with many men. For these reasons she will be divorced.

Her fear was mainly about life for her and the children. A few women were afraid of the finances as they were totally dependent on their husbands. Some women shared that the land and the house is in the name of the husband who has the right to give it to anyone he likes; the dependent wife and the children will have no place to stay if they are thrown out of the house. One of the reasons for not sharing with others was that she feared whether confidentiality will be maintained. A feeling of shame was also a reason.

CHART 13

Persons Approached by Abused Womens for Help

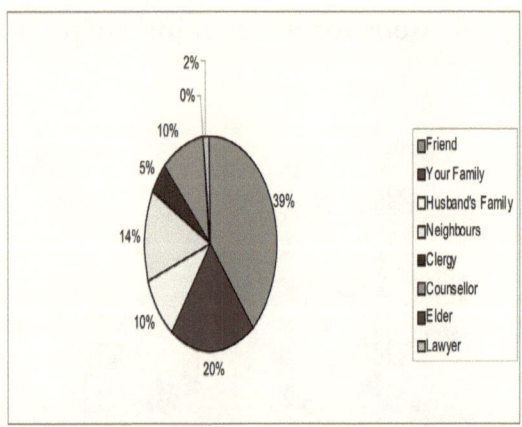

The majority of the abused women sought help after facing abuse. Help sought was from friends, families, clergy, and counselors. The help was mostly received from childhood friends who gave them an opportunity to share their sorrows. They felt that the friends are caring, understanding and trustworthy. The victims were confident that they would not share these matters with others. At the same time they hoped that these friends might find means and ways of solving problems. They felt more comfortable to share the most intimate matters with a person very close to them from childhood because they did not accuse the abused women as being the cause of the abuse. These friends provided shelter for the victim and her children. Many said that their friends were non-Christians. Therefore they received only emergency help and not any Biblical help. Only a very few abused women approached clergy for help. These few were rural women. Not a single abused woman from an urban area sought help from clergy. One of the reasons was that they met the clergy only on Sundays at the church or because they are busy people. They feel that clergies are strangers. Women were not comfortable to share matters with a total stranger. The abused women thought that it would be of no use if they shared the matter of abuse with a clergy as he may not be equipped to deal with the situation or that they were less interested to listen to the problem and offer to help in emergency situations. A few said that after listening to the illustrations commonly uses by the clergy during the sermon, women felt uncomfortable to share about the issue of abuse. They feared that he may use their family problem as an illustration in the sermon. This would not help in anyway. This tendency of clergy has lost the confidentiality among the abusers and the abused.

CHART 14
Persons Approached Abused Womens for Help in Urban and Rural Areaas

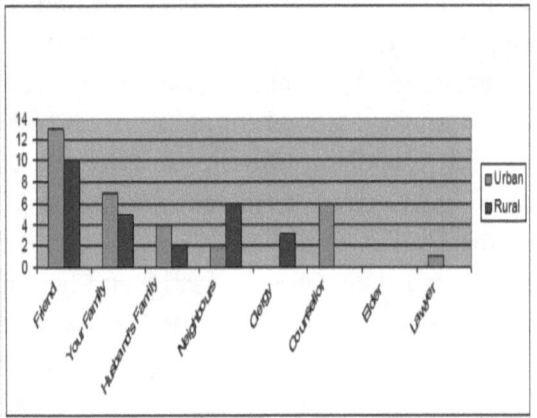

During the time of interaction with the abused women the researcher asked whom they approached for any type of assistance. The answer was quite surprising. For 39 % of abused women, intimate friends or friends from childhood were the solace most of the time. The reasons for this are that their intimate friends or friends from childhood keep confidentiality. Their friendship and the dilemma faced by their close friend are more important than gossip. Their difficulty is important and they want to see a suitable solution to their problems. These friends listen to their troubles with much sympathy and compassion.

Though most of them are habitual church goers, only 5% of them approached the clergy directly, that too from the rural area. More details are given in table 3, 'reasons that hinders an abused woman from approaching the clergy.'

Rural women were more reluctant to seek help when compared with their urban counterparts. The reasons may be financial dependency, cultural influences, lower educational level, lack of proper knowledge and awareness about the help available for the victims. Rural women, due to financial dependency and with no help from outsiders decided to 'hang on' to the husband in spite of abuse. They did not want to complicate the matters by seeking help. A few urban and rural women approached their own family members and those of the husband's family. Nobody sought help from church elders.

CHART 15

Advice/Help Received

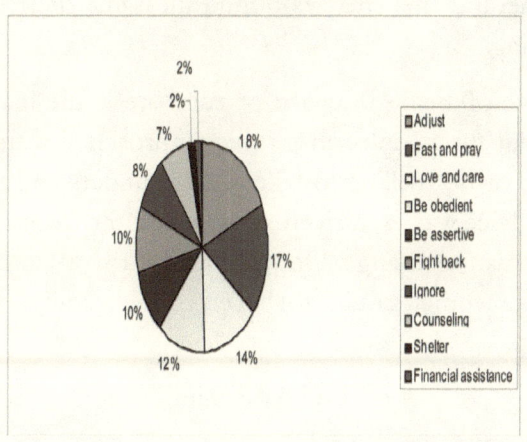

The author learned that most of the women were given advice when they approached their friends, neighbours, family and clergy. However, much advice consisted of 'helpless' responses like adjust, fast and pray, love and care, be obedient, ignore, which did not change the situation for the abusee. This advice was of no use or made the situation even worse. Counseling, offering shelter and financial assistance may have proven effective and practical.

The majority of the women said that their families advised them to adjust with the husband and the situation, for the stability and continuity of the marriage.

A few urban women who were employed and better educated said that they approached a counselor and later a lawyer. Most of the women said that they tolerated the abuse to a great extent. It was when things went beyond limits that the matter was shared with others. They tried different methods to reduce abuse by fasting and praying, trying to be more affectionate and obedient. Hence the advice received from others was a repetition of what had been already tried earlier.

Advice like being assertive, fight back or to ignore has often worsened the situation rather than improving it. A different response occurs as a practice in rural areas. Either the wife's family, local influential people or the clergy threaten the husband and request that he stop the abuse. As a result the husband stops the abuse for a short period of time and then may continue the same. Perhaps he needs another warning.

Irrespective of being in urban or rural areas, the majority of the women felt that the people whom they approached were biased; not spending time or not willing to take time to understand the situation. Worse, their advice was exclusively centered on the woman, not usually on asking the man to change. On the whole it is very disheartening to learn that these women could not receive timely advice, wise counsel or proper help.

CHART 16

Views on Responsibility of Clergy

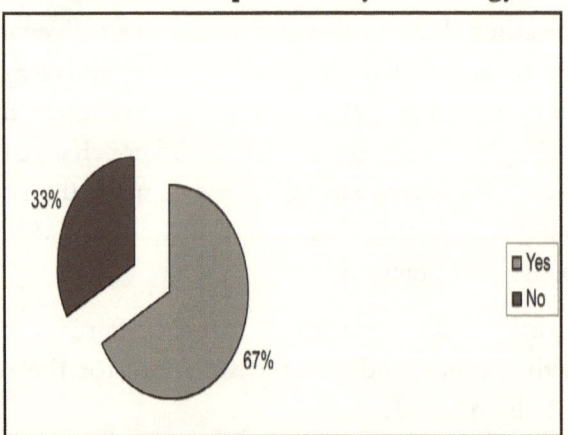

Sixty seven percent agreed that clergy and the church have an important role in dealing with abuse within the church and society. At present they do not do it properly or genuinely. The reasons are that the church can address the important issue of abuse by speaking and teaching from Biblical principles. A few women said that the church should hold the abusers responsible for their actions, should intervene, and confront them.

Role of Clergy and Church to Reduce the Abuse of Women

The methods to act in keeping with the role of clergy and church, to help to reduce the abuse of women, according to the preference of the respondents are given below. These are the views shared by the married women. When clergy were questioned similarly, their preferred rank differed. This is shown in table 11

TABLE 2

Preferred rank	Role of clergy
1.	Strong pulpit preaching and teaching on Christian marriage and family.
2.	Condemning wrong deeds.
3.	Regular home visits by clergy and elders.
4.	Strengthening fellowship.
5.	Arranging family seminars.
6.	Creating support groups.
7.	Church discipline.
8.	Counseling
9.	Pre-marital counseling
10.	Raise women's self esteem.
11.	Referral services
12.	Financial support
13.	Rehabilitation

Reasons that Hinder an Abused Woman from Approaching Clergy

The majority of women said that clergy have no time for the congregation or the church families as they are mostly occupied with various activities in the church (health care programme and developmental activities, administration, supervision of construction, committees and church planting.) They have less time for pastoral care and counseling due to this. The clergy and church committees need to prioritize things. They need to focus more on spiritual activities than on developmental activities.

Others feel that clergy have a tendency or inclination to include confidential matters shared during counseling as illustrations in sermons. Hence the respondents felt that most of the clergy could not maintain confidentiality. They also expressed the view that clergy are total strangers, so how could they share matters of a confidential nature. A few said that some clergy are not adequately trained to handle situations of violence against women or any unforeseen crisis that comes in their ministry.

Clergy can also become unpopular; the church members may not be pleased about the clergy getting involved in this kind of issue. At times the decision can be biased.

The list below shows the perceptions of the respondents.

TABLE 3

Preferred rank	Reasons for not approaching clergy
1.	Clergy have no time for the congregation
2.	Clergy usually don't maintain confidentiality
3.	Clergy may not be adequately trained to handle the situation
4.	Clergy are meant for church related activities only
5.	Cultural displeasure
6.	Lay people may not like it
7.	Counsellors are better equipped
8.	Clergy can become unpopular

CHART 17

Tolerance to Abuse

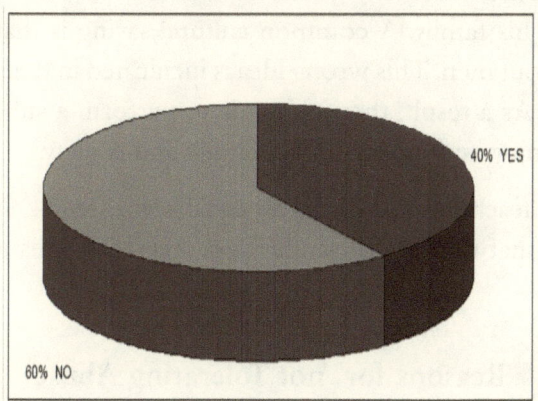

Whether living in urban or rural areas, employed or non-employed or unemployed, graduates or non-graduates, most of the women took time to answer this question: 'do you think a wife should tolerate abuse'? Sixty percent of the respondents vehemently expressed that women should not have to tolerate abuse though many of them were experiencing abuse. The rest of them had a mindset to tolerate abuse due to various reasons which are explained in chart 19. The researcher thinks that they had some reservations in answering this question.

CHART 18

Reasons for Tolerating Abuse

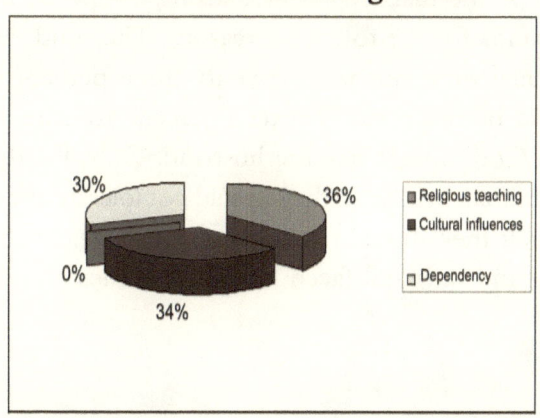

It was learned that thirty-four percent of the women tolerated abuse for cultural reasons. The cultural influence made them believe that their only responsibility in the family is to look after their husband, children and his family. A common cultural saying is that women are nobody without men. This wrong idea is inculcated in their minds from a young age. As a result, they are made to perform a subordinate role while men enjoy supremacy in the family and society.

Religious teachings had an almost equal influence (34%). Thirty-four percent said that they are dependent on their husbands in all aspects.

CHART 19

Reasons for not Tolerating Abuse

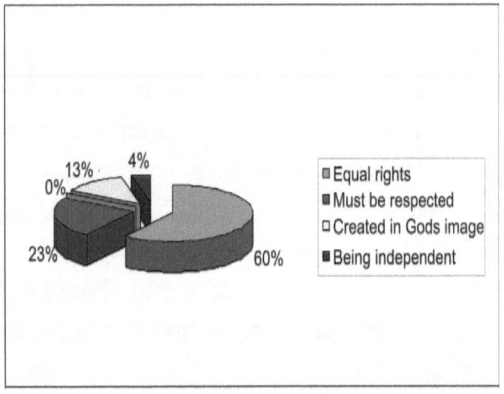

Sixty percent of the married women strongly opposed being abused by their husbands for the following reasons. They said that they have equal rights like their husband. Twenty-three percent believe that women should be respected. Thirteen percent are sure that they are also made in God's image like the husband. Only 4% think they are independent human beings, so they should not tolerate abuse. However, though they felt they should not tolerate abuse, nearly all the women did tolerate it and they still faced it in their homes.

Analysis of the Responses from Clergy

One hundred clergies were the subject of this study. In one denomination, there are lady clergy as well. Sixty percent of the surveyed clergy were working in urban and 40% in rural parishes. They were selected through the contacts of the researcher and his friends.

The denomination details are given below.

TABLE 4

Sl.No	Denomination	Urban	Rural	Total
1	Church of South India / Church of North India	18	02	20
2	St Thomas Evangelical Church of India (STECI)	02	08	10
3	Catholic Church	08	02	10
4	Seventh Day Adventist Church	03	07	10
5	Syrian Marthoma Church	05	05	10
6	Brethren Church	05	00	05
7	Pentecostal Church	02	08	10
8	Assemblies of God	05	00	05
9	Syrian Orthodox Church	07	03	10
10	Evangelical Church of India	00	05	05
11	Methodist Church	05	00	05

Period of Ordination

TABLE 5

Years	Number of respondents
0 – 5	07
5 – 10	09
10 – 15	32
15 – 20	17
20 – 25	10
25 – 30	19
30 and above years	06

The majority of the clergy had 10–15 years of pastoral experience after theological studies. Even though the majority had been ordained for more than ten years, the anecdotal evidence during the interviews made the researchers think that they were not confident to intervene in family crisis situations in their respect.

CHART 20
Pastoral Experience after Theological Studies

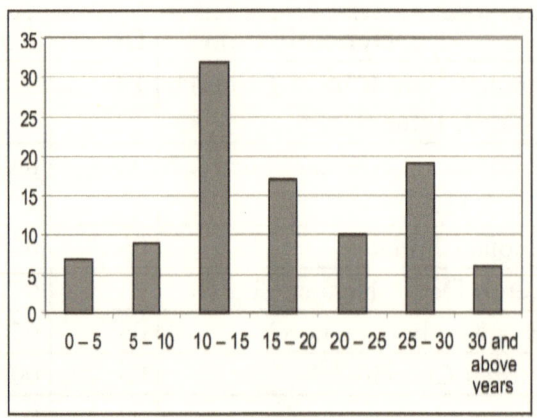

CHART 21
Theological Background

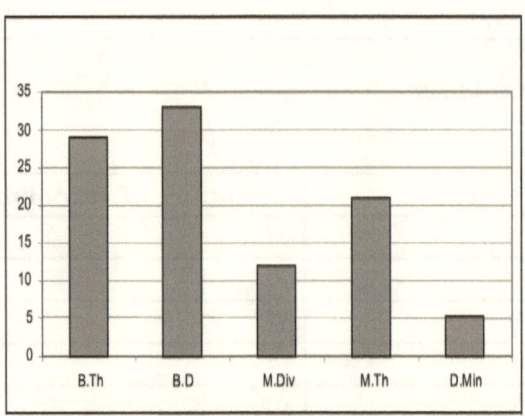

The theological training of the clergy varied from B.Th to D.Min. Twenty-two of them had extra educational qualifications like B.A,

B. Ed, L.LB, M.A etc. along with theological studies. Some of the respondents had done higher studies abroad. A few worked as faculty in theological schools and colleges.

TABLE 6

Number of Families in the Parish

Approximate number of families	Number of clergy respondents
Below 25	10
25 – 50	31
50 – 75	32
75 – 100	08
100 – 150	08
150 – 500	06
500 – 1000	03
1000 – 1500	02

32% of the clergy had 50 – 75 families in their parish; 31% had 20-25 families. There were parishes with 1000 – 1500 families too. Some clergy have responsibilities of more than 3 – 4 parishes when the number of families in each parish is less than 10. Commuting to different parishes took much time for these clergy.

CHART 22

Number of Clergy Respondents

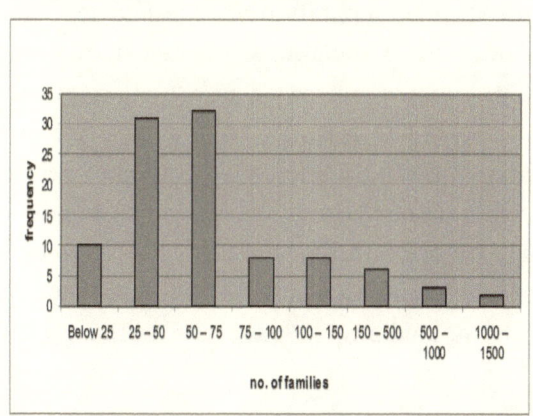

Have Clergy come across Abuse of Women in their Parish?

Irrespective of the denominations, the majority of the respondents agreed that abuse of women exists in Christian families and also in their respective parishes even though they cannot specify the exact number of cases. Some said it was not so. They said that a person who is born-again cannot abuse another person in their family, but they agreed with the researcher that at times, verbal or psychological abuse may happen knowingly or unknowingly.

CHART 23
Source of Information about Abuse of Women

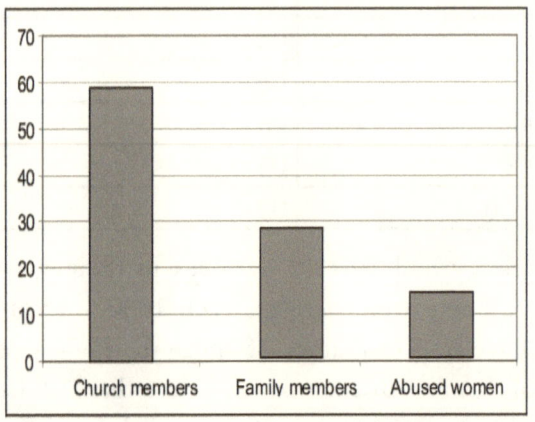

Clergy revealed that a few women approached the clergy directly, due to the fact that they were unable to tolerate the abuse any more or have reached the stage of separation or even suicide. Otherwise mostly the parents or relatives of the abused women shared the burden with the clergy, but the major source of information to them was from the church members. The majority of the cases informed to clergy concerned physical abuse. There were instances reported where a few women were not allowed by their husbands to attend the cottage prayer meetings or the Sunday worship service. Even then he was not sure whether the families wanted him to intervene or not. Unless specified he was not willing to intervene because he thought that the situation had gone beyond control and that corrective steps may not be possible at that juncture. This was shared by a few clergymen during the interview.

CHART 24
Role of Clergy to Reduce abuse of Women

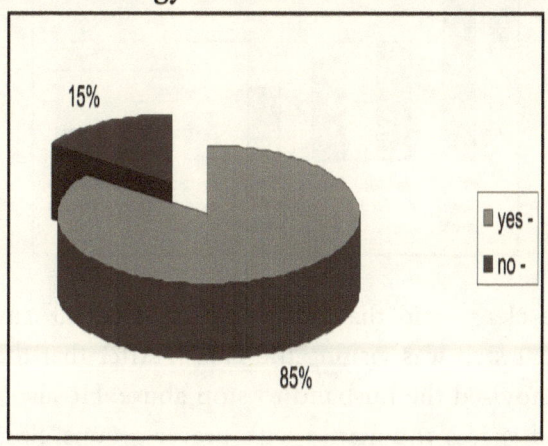

Eighty-five percent of the clergy agreed that they have a major and significant role to play to reduce, prevent or bring to an end abuse of women in Christian families. Some are happy to do that, but some of them do not know how it is possible. Fifteen percent said that there is no role for clergy in reducing abuse of women. These clergy are less experienced individuals. Out of these fifteen percent, a few respondents said that when there are qualified professionals who can deal with this issue they need not unnecessarily interfere. Others expressed the opinion that meeting spiritual needs is the most important responsibility of clergy. The clergy have a role to educate abusers, and bring repentance in their lives.

CHART 25
Handling the Situation of Abuse of Women

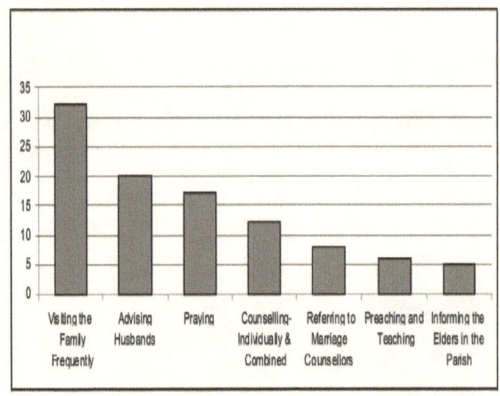

Most of the clergy said that once they received information about abuse, the first step was visiting the family. After that the clergy said they usually advised the husband to stop abuse. He also spends time in prayer and shares the matter with prayer groups. Some members of the prayer group visit the family and hold prayer meetings. Some of the clergy said that neither was the abusee comfortable to share the whole experience with a group of people who were inquisitive, nor was comfortable for the abuser to have a group of people hearing about his abuse. If the severity of abuse or the situation was very bad, clergy called them for counseling, individually or together. And if the situation was still worse, the clergy referred the spouses to marriage counselors. A few of the clergy said that when it happened in affluent families, there was a difficulty in approaching the family or telling the wrongness of abuse directly to the husband. The researcher recognizes it as a mere excuse of the clergy rather than a genuine reason.

TABLE 7

Subjects studied during Theological Education with regard to Christian Family

Subject	Yes	No
Issues faced by the Christians	89	11
Christian home	92	8
Christian marriage	95	5
Crisis management	39	61
Family counseling	45	55
Inter-personal relationship	17	83
Social and ethical issues	45	55
Family finances	32	68
Laws of marriage	41	59

The table indicates that the majority of the clergy have been taught about having a Christian home and family during their theological studies. Nevertheless they admitted that they did not have sufficient lectures to learn to intervene in family crisis situations. The instruction received during the theological training was apparently not enough, not appropriate for the modern age and not very practical. They admitted that they did not have practical training to acquire better counseling skills to deal with abuse. Yet most of them are confident that their theological education was sufficient to carry out ministerial activities effectively. Some clergy shared that when they tried to use the theory they had learned to solve crisis situations, they ended in failure and with more complications. Some said that their life experiences helped them a lot to deal with the issue of abuse.

In contrast, women respondents had said that clergymen are not adequately trained to handle the crisis. This is depicted in table 3.

CHART 26
Inadequacy of Clergy in Training

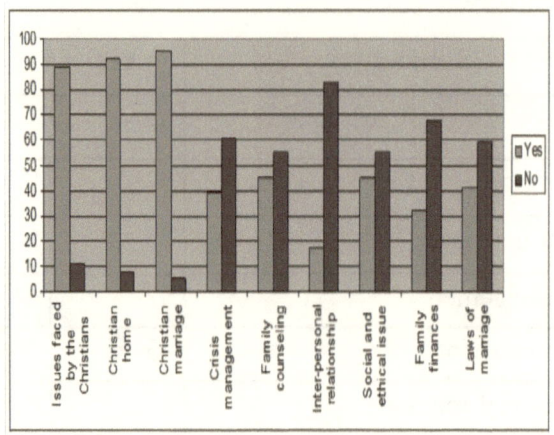

Even though some of the clergy studied in the same theological college in the same academic year, they responded differently about the subjects taught. This is reported as the researcher knows these clergy personally. One woman clergy shared that she learned these topics with great interest, viewed this issue with concern and expressed that they have a great responsibility to prevent abuse of women.

Whether Theological Training helped Clergy in Reducing Abuse?

The clergy with more than twenty years of pastoral experience shared that the experience acquired as a clergy had helped them in dealing with abuse of women. They are mature enough to diagnose the problem due to their vast experience. Though a few relevant topics are incorporated in the curriculum, they need to be equipped with adequate practical knowledge and skills to deal with the modern generation.

CHART 27

Help of Theological Training in Dealing with Abuse

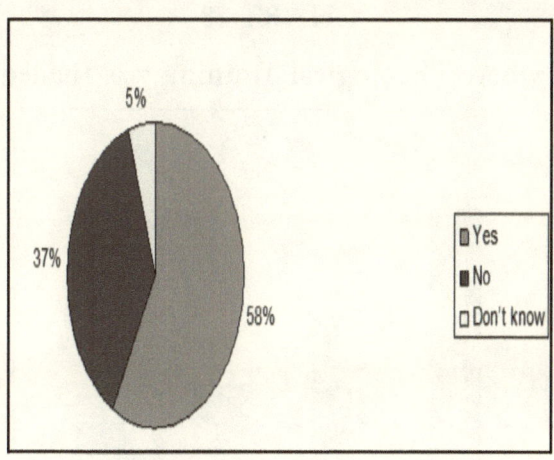

Thirty-seven percent of the clergy said that they cannot handle abuse and they strongly felt that the lack of specific teaching on abuse and lack of practical training were the hindrances; five percent did not want to take the risk by interfering in the matter of abuse. This was due to the sincere feeling that they were not proficient and skilled to help the women in crisis and to tide over the trauma. Some conveniently did nothing, fearing displeasure of the parish members.

Area where the Theological Training was Inadequate in Dealing with Abuse

CHART 28

Area where Theological Training was Inadequate

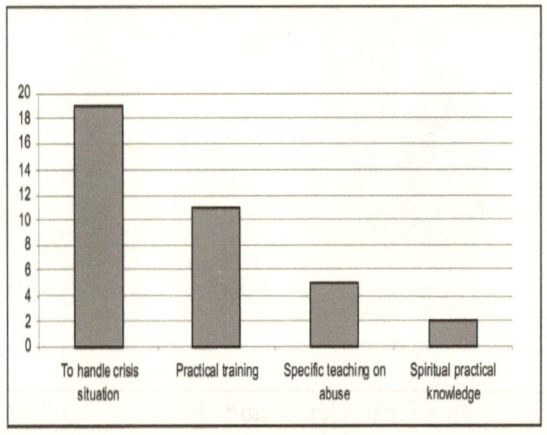

Fifty-one percent of the clergy revealed that their theological training had failed to train them on crisis situations in families; thirty percent of the clergy said that they lacked practical training in handling abuse; 14% were of the opinion that there were no specific biblical teachings on abuse. Hence it need not be considered as their responsibility. Respondents with less than five years of experience after ordination reported that they were lacking spiritual practical knowledge.

TABLE 8

Assistance that the Clergy Seek when Unable to Handle the Situation Alone

Senior clergy	53
Wife	19
Elders	06
Marriage counselors	08
Books	03
Church discipline	11

CHART 29
Help Sought when Unable to Handle the Situation

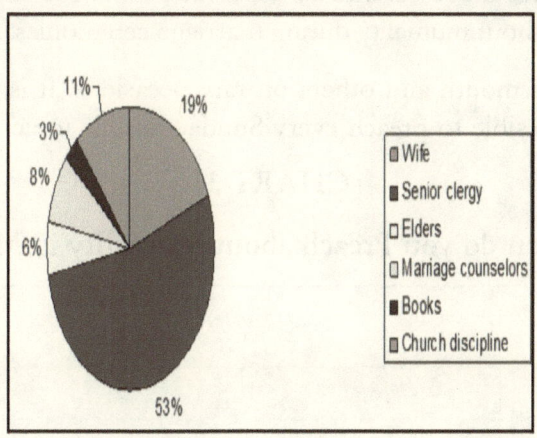

Nearly half (53%) of the clergy acknowledged that they sought the help or advice from senior clergy when they were unable to handle the abuse situation alone; 19% of the clergy shared the matters with their wives and considered their opinion; 11% of the clergy said that they implemented church policies to discipline the abuser when the matter of abuse is brought to their notice. They considered it as a serious offence. Eight percent said that they referred the case to a marriage counselor.

CHART 30
Do you Preach about Mutuality in Marriage?

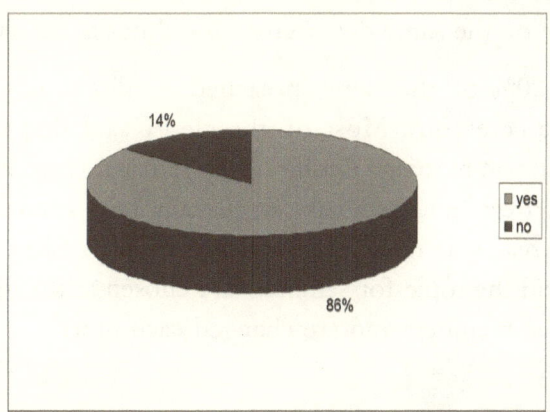

Eighty-six percent of the clergy said that they preached about mutuality in marriage, whereas fourteen percent said that they don't preach about it. Nevertheless the researcher has reservations in believing this. Clergy may preach about mutuality during marriage ceremonies. Some others

do so once a month and others on rare occasions. It is difficult and almost impossible to preach every Sunday on this topic.

CHART 31

How often do you Preach about Mutuality in Marriage?

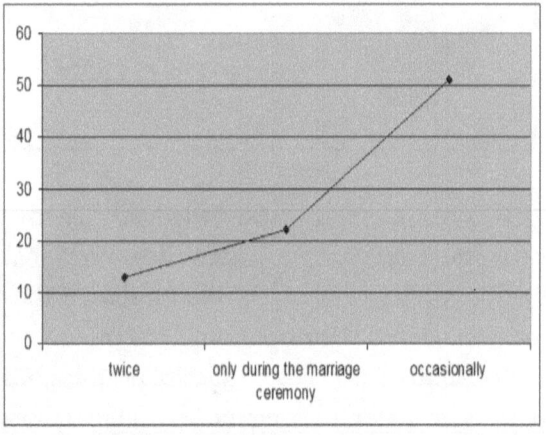

The sermon topic for the Sunday worship service is prepared by the church through the almanac and normally clergy do not opt to change it. A few clergy said that at least twice a year they preached on mutuality in marriage as it is incorporated in the church almanac. However some of the clergy of the same denomination did not agree with it.

Around 20% of the clergy preached on this topic only during the marriage ceremony. Most of the clergy said that they preach about mutuality in marriage during family retreats, seminars and other programs. Retreats and seminars are usually held annually in urban parishes whereas it is rarely conducted in rural parishes. Theme for the retreat and the topic for seminars are chosen at the discretion of the committee members and are changed each time.

Barriers to Teach or Preach on Abuse of Women in Christian Families

This was an open question to the clergy to narrate the hindrances they faced in preaching and teaching on abuse according to their preferences. The ranking is done by preferences.

TABLE 9
Barriers to Teach or Preach
on Abuse of Women in Christian Families

Preferred rank	Hindrances
1	Not enough time due to various activities
2	Not adequately trained to handle the situation
3	Cultural displeasure
4	Can become unpopular
5	Lay people may not like it
6	Counselors are better equipped than clergy
7	Clergy is meant for church related activities only

Steps to Overcome Barrier / Hindrances in Preaching and Teaching against Abuse of Women

This question was asked to the clergy for suggesting the steps to overcome the barriers for preaching on abuse according to their preferences. The ranking is done by preference.

Preferred rank	Steps to overcome these barriers
1	Hold seminars, retreats regularly
2	Create awareness among the parish members
3	Interacting with parish committee
4	Understand that the process of change is time consuming

Effective Ways for Reducing the Abuse of Women

This was an open question to the clergy to recommend how to effectively reduce the abuse of women according to their preferences. The ranking is done accordingly.

TABLE 10

Effective Ways for Reducing the Abuse of Women

Preferred rank	Effective ways
1	Regular home visits by clergy and elders
2	Arranging family seminars
3	Strengthening fellowship
4	Strong pulpit preaching and teaching on Christian marriage and family
5	Condemning wrong deeds
6	Church discipline
7	Raise women's self esteem
8	Pre-marital counseling
9	Counseling
10	Creating support groups for women
11	Referral services
12	Financial support
13	Rehabilitation

The married women want the clergy to teach and preach from the pulpit which they believe is the effective way to reduce abuse (table 2). Surprisingly the clergy prioritized this to fourth when compared to the other ways of reducing abuse. One of the views of clergy was that the sermon topics are given by the authorities as per the church almanac. They are constrained to preach accordingly. So these topics on Christian family, mutuality, inter-personal relationship, and how to handle money cannot be preached on a regular basis. In contrast, the women think that the sermons can change the attitude and behavior of the abusers.

Chapter 6

Recommendations

A s we express our gratitude, we must never forget that the highest appreciation is not to utter words, but to live by them. *John F. Kennedy*

Abuse is a sinful behavior, which dominates or controls other individual. Only prayers, genuine repentance, sincere homework, forgiveness and reconciliation with the influence of the Holy Spirit can heal the wound of abuse permanently.

Dignity and respect are the two key ethical principles of the Human Rights Act. Being treated with dignity and respect improves an individual's self-respect, self-worth, courage, and productivity. Any movement against this invites loneliness, depression, shame and low self-image. When an individual's dignity is questioned or compromised at anytime in front of children, relatives, friends or domestic helpers, there is no doubt it is considered as abuse thus attacking the rights of individual. All these elements can change one's personal life and in turn change the challenges in marital life.

The Apostle Peter admonishes to "...live in harmony with one another, be sympathetic, love...be compassionate and humble." (1 Peter 3:8). The Apostle Paul says along with Peter, "...one in spirit and purpose." Oneness plays a great role in the unity and stability of any human relationship, especially in the marital relationship.

Following are recommendation based on the interaction that the researcher had that included interviews, and questionnaires completed by members of the church and clergy. The recommendations are categorized as the roles of clergy, church, and the theological schools / colleges / seminaries. All these agencies can play a vital role in their own ways and collectively in ensuring a reduction, prevention or elimination of abuse of women.

The Role of Clergy

A member of the clergy must be a caring, loving, empathetic and compassionate individual. He must be a man of vision, mission and action: a prayerful warrior, problem solver, an able teacher, good communicator, good decision maker, good leader and lead an exemplary family life. He must recognize the genuineness of the situation of abuse, intervene at the right time in the right way and render appropriate help both physically and spiritually. He should always be prepared for crisis intervention if the need arises with the help of his team. For that he must have the ability to handle the crisis situation in an amicable way. Sometimes quick action may be necessary.

Compared to modern times, the clergy of yester years had more time with people and they were willing to spend time with their congregation. People had more confidence and trust in the clergy of the past than they do in the present. I wouldn't like to give any impression that the clergy of this era are lazy or do not do their job as expected. They are more theologically educated and well qualified. In the olden times the clergy used their power and authority given by the Almighty God to rebuke, if needed; otherwise they counseled them to overcome the mistakes of the perpetrator. Now-a-days the pastor is afraid to do so as this is a sensitive issue and he knows that the committee members or the members of the congregation may not support him getting involved. He will conveniently recommend them to a marriage counselor for help with the pretext that he is busy.

Shepherding the Flock

It is a general understanding that the clergy conduct religious rituals, worship services, manage institutions, supervise building projects, attend umpteen number of meetings, perform social services and participate in church related activities. A pastor or priest is considered to be a very busy person. Having engaged and busy with multiple tasks, abused women may not be sure whether he is the right person with whom they could share their problems or whether he will have time to listen to a person who needs help. A few women who were economically poor felt that the clergy are only for the rich and influential people in the church. There are many who doubted whether clergy are adequately trained to deal with the issue of abuse though they are energetic speakers. Some abused women are under the impression that since majority of the clergy are male, they support only husbands.

It was distressing to listen to a few respondents who stated that they considered clergies as strangers as they see them only on Sundays or during important function at church and some of them refrain from mingling with the members of his congregation.

The clergy should give full attention to the spiritual aspects of the church rather than executing other assignments. Clergy should seek assistance if the number of parish members is much more than he or she can handle and their activities have greatly increased. Clergy must take the initiative to update their knowledge and develop their counselling skills to deal with current issues of abuse.

Preaching and Teaching

Clergy should preach and teach regularly on mutual submission, equality and mutuality in Christian marriage, family, home, stewardship, conflict management, crisis management, fruits of the Spirit and so on. Further, the clergy must teach through preaching or counselling about responsibility, accountability, developing self-control, self-discipline, consistency in prayer life, transparency in communication, appreciating each other, showing respect to the partner, and the value of a healthy and meaningful family life. The practical aspect can be emphasised incorporating it along with the assigned topic. Extra marital affairs should never happen in a sanctified Christian marriage.

An effective sermon from the pulpit does not come automatically. It needs hard work, sacrifice, effort, constant labour and above all the blessings of Lord Almighty. According to Earl V Comfort, there are seven qualities, which the pulpit makes more effective.[1]

- Preaching must be biblical; Bible rooted.

- It must be understandable. Use every available source to communicate the Bible effectively.

- It must be warm. According to Lloyd Jones,to love to preach is one thing; to love whom you preach is quite another.[2]

- It must be positive; when people leave church, they have to go with a positive attitude toward God.

- It must be practical; he has to concentrate more on the practical side of the problem.

- It must be exemplary; he must preach what he practices by being an example to others.

- It must be exciting; Lloyd-Jones wrote like this, a dull preacher is a contradiction in terms; if he is dull, he is not a preacher.[3]

It is true that not all clergy can be like John Wesley, Dwight L. Moody, Spurgeon or Billy Graham, but they can strive for improvement with the help of the Holy Spirit and through the constant study of the word of God, prayer life and hard work.

The message must be based on the centrality of the person and work of Jesus Christ. As John Calvin held, the apostles' preaching contained nothing but Christ alone. Paul's message is Christ centered. This must be the ultimate aim of every servant of God to present Jesus Christ to his people. Paul preached the message of Christ very clearly and with full of confidence. He assures the Corinthians that, when he presented them with the Gospel, he did so by setting forth the truth plainly. The truth must be presented to the people in an intelligible and in a practical way. The clergy ought to minister to their people under divine compulsion and not rely on their knowledge or ability.

Counselling

Counselling is an art and a science. Christian counselling should be done prayerfully with the guidance of the Holy Spirit based on the biblical truths. The main purpose of pastoral care and counselling is to restore broken relationships and to help people who are going through a crisis.

The following are the unique features in pastoral counselling when compared with any other counselling. In pastoral counselling, one can experience the presence of the God, and the guidance of the Holy Spirit. That gives a confidence and prevents lonely feelings. The most important factor in pastoral counselling is that one starts and ends with prayer. That means we give glory and honour to God Almighty. One seeks God's guidance and leading in the counselling session. In pastoral counselling, the Word of God is a valuable tool. This will give assurance to the counselee that whatever is being done is based on God's word and not on one's own understanding. A well-trained pastoral counselor should have a good knowledge of sociology, philosophy, theology, ethics, psychology, legal aspects and current affairs. Such knowledge will be an additional help in the life and ministry of a pastor who is engaged in counselling.

"There are many who are mentally and spiritually hurt in our society. These people need love, care, hope, assurance, encouragement and support. These can be achieved successfully through the ministry of counselling, as it is a one to one relationship. Pastoral counselling sheds fresh light in the dark areas in the counselee's life."[4]

From the life of David (Psalms 23), we understand his cry to the great counsellor and affirm, He restores my soul. The good shepherd 'strengthen' and 'heals innermost being.' (Ezekiel 34:4, 16). "The weak individual needs strengthening by encouraging words, sick need physical or emotional healing- the crippled need binding up, and those who are strained need attention to bring them back to the fold."[5]

The activities of pastoral care include ethical advice, offering prayers, guidance, counselling and ritual observances. Sometimes guiding them to an NGO for financial assistance, finding accommodation facilities for those who need long stay, transportation, assistance at hospital becomes an added responsibility. Being with them during difficult times is very important. Encourage them with edifying words using apt words at the right time is also important.

Ministerial ethics absolutely demand that the clergy must be prepared to keep the secrets of counseling and not indulge in gossip in any manner and he should never use the incident as an illustration. There may be situations where he would like to discuss a particular difficulty, with his spouse or with an experienced senior clergy. But he should ensure that whatever matter is told to them must be kept confidential.

During interview, a few women expressed that they cannot trust the clergy completely as they do not maintain confidentiality. The incident shared to the clergy may be used as an illustration in sermons or sometimes shared with other people in the congregation. Too often people use this as a revenge-tactic on others. Although he may be quoting this with good intention so that others won't repeat this abuse, it may cause different repercussions. It is sometimes felt that clergy are not mature enough to deal with the issues. In recent years plenty of allegations have been made against the clergy - sexual or social abuse against women who came for help. Therefore the abused women do not have any confidence in clergy. Their arguments are; Why I should go for further abuse? Enough is enough.

Many times we come across a woman being counseled and her male counterpart does not attend the sessions. One sided counseling cannot be considered as good counselling. There are several questions like who to adjust or yield - what to adjust, where to adjust, how to adjust, and how far to adjust? Can few simple adjustments without any real repentance solve the problem? Adjustment or compromise has to be from both sides. Mutual adjustments by both the spouses are required for solving the problem. Asking only to a woman to change means she is at fault. She is blamed and becomes the root cause of the abuse. If only the woman needs to make the adjustment, only she will continue to suffer the abuse as the husband is not willing to change his behavior. So the term adjustment should be a mutual adjustment.

The husband and the wife should be counseled individually and then together, depending upon the severity of the abuse. If the abuse is severe then never call them jointly, rather call them individually. This makes it easier to tackle the situation. The husband must be given sufficient time to change. If he is not willing to listen or work for a change, then call him before the church committee and warn him. Withdraw his active church membership and never allow him to serve the church in any committee in any capacity until and unless there is a positive change in his marital relationship.

The author highlights the need for effective pre-marital counseling for a minimum period of three months for giving insight into a stable married life. The topic of marriage, family life, spirituality, sexual life, managing a home, family budget, and handling family finances is to be thoroughly discussed before marriage. This must be followed by post-marital counselling sessions. A series of studies regarding this matter is essential for a long-lasting, happy marital life.

Home Visits

Ministering from the pulpit and home visits are to be considered equally important for the clergy. No pastor can ignore the ministry of house visits. Visiting women and men of all age groups who are sick, those with terminal illnesses, those who are in the hospital, those with financial stress, who are hurt, depressed, or bereaved is important. Women and children who were regularly attending church, but not doing so of late, are to be followed up along with the senior citizens who are unable to attend the church services due to ill health, lack of transportation, lack of a proper escort, or who are not able to attend lengthy worship services. They will gladly welcome the pastoral visit for spiritual fellowship, sharing their concerns, encouragement and for an enriching time with the clergy. The house visits may help the clergy to understand why they do not come to church. Once we find out the reasons, it becomes easier to bring them back to the church to have fellowship with others.

The clergy must visit those in sorrow and those who are troubled emotionally, physically, and spiritually and the backsliders (James 5:20). Such visits will encourage and strengthen people in their spiritual life. During these visits, the clergy can give proper guidance and advice for better living and minister to the spiritual hunger of the people, so that their Christian walk will be more meaningful, fruitful and effective for themselves and for others.

What are the outcomes of home visits? A true and healthy relationship is built up and a foundation laid for future ministry. It enables the clergy to weep with those are weeping, to provide comfort and offer moral support during times of trouble or illness, to provide a living faith in times of crisis, and to stimulate spiritual and emotional growth. It also, builds confidence in the life of the people. A house visit is a time of fellowship. The pastor should strive to create a genial atmosphere. He should not be talking all the time; family members must be encouraged express themselves. Sometimes preconceived ideas that could have got into the mind of clergy due to gossip of other members make the pastor focus only on one angle but fail to understand the holistic aspect. Thus by listening to them the pastor can guide them and plan strategies to help them overcome their problems.

It gives an opportunity for the pastor to see the needs in different areas in their life. By listening to what the family members have to say, the pastor could perhaps guide them and devise strategies to help them. It provides the pastor a close affinity with the families of his congregation. It gives him an idea of their spiritual level, values and standards and their priorities in Christian life. It also helps the pastor analyze and plan new ways of meeting the needs of the congregation.

Based on the feedback and observations, he can develop new strategies or perspectives so he can deliver sermon more effectively. It also builds and fosters interpersonal relationships. It can motivate the people to come to church regularly, as they feel wanted.

It makes the family grow much stronger in faith during testing times as the pastor is like a shepherd who goes after the lost sheep and guides the family during times of crisis through prayer and spiritual insights. During these visits he should be able to observe and find out if there are issues of abuse. He should create such an atmosphere, assuring confidentiality so that the women can freely share the problems. He should insist on family prayers, studying the word of God and having fellowship with God's children.

Creating Awareness

The primary factor in preventing or reducing abuse is to recognize and understand that abuse of women by their spouses prevails in Indian Christian families irrespective of the denomination, locality, education, language, culture, and financial status. Clergy have to identify the fact that abuse of women occurs in their own respective parishes. Clergy should create awareness among the members of the church about the existence and the extent of abuse as well as the seriousness and its effect on families and the church's role in reducing or preventing abuse of women. This could be done through pulpit preaching, teaching, group or personal discussions. Clergy can use occasions like retreats or seminars to teach about the injustice of abuse and the Biblical views. Some local churches, clergy, and counselors fail to address abuse face-to-face for fear of breaking up a marriage. Others steer clear of addressing the topic from the pulpit or in adult education for fear of broaching an uncomfortable subject. This silence around domestic violence has to end. In togetherness we can fight against this evil so that the peace of our God prevails in all our families.

Action Plan by the Clergy

Clergy should also realize their role and responsibilities in preventing abuse against women. In order to prepare themselves for this, clergy ought to lead a God centered life, leading an exemplary family life. Apostle Paul states the same in 1 Timothy 3:2-5. The pastor should always be a role model as a spiritual leader in front of his family and society. His exemplary family life will help him take the initiative in dealing with the abuse of women. The virtues of integrity, honesty, assertiveness and genuineness and being impartial should be developed and practiced by the clergy. His wife should also assist him in the ministry.

Anytime the clergy get information that a woman is abused by her husband occasionally or constantly, the clergy should have an action plan and take steps prudently, secretly and prayerfully to prevent or eliminate the abuse and to bring restoration in the life of the abuser.

The step a clergy can take is to remind, reassure and encourage the woman of her worth and value before God. The extent and the severity of the crisis must be discerned properly and wisely. If the couple is separated, the woman and the children should be protected as much as possible. If need arises essential and suitable referrals for the victims should be arranged. Observe if any life threatening situation prevails. The victim and victimizer must be directed and led to God who is the source of restoration, reconciliation, peace, comfort and the provider of inner healing.

The clergy should assess the situation very sensitively and carefully and find out whether what she is saying is genuine or not. Then the question comes, How can you know that what is saying is true? He can gather information about abuse from the woman's relatives, close or intimate friends, from her work area, or from the immediate family members or even from her children.

Find out if there are any minor or major reasonable visible marks or injuries on her body during these periods of abuse, whether she had been admitted during this period to any hospital for treatment for minor or major injuries caused by physical or emotional abuse. A medical or psychological evaluation is highly advisable, depending upon the situation. A competent team can assist the pastor.

Through counseling try to convince the abuser that what he is doing is wrong in the sight of God, in front of children, friends and relatives. Regular moral support of the victim is needed to a great extent because of isolation, rejection, denial and humiliation.

Victim must be advised to maintain a documentation of events of abuse from day one for future reference if the need arises. This will give legitimate feedback as to how often the incidence of abuse took place in her life, rather than guess work, gossip or creating unnecessary allegation against the spouse.

Make sure that the woman and her children are under the safe custody, in case she has to leave home alone or with the children. She should set apart enough finances and pack clothes, significant documents, and telephone numbers or postal addresses of a few important people who could be of help to her. She should also think of a home where she can take temporary refuge. The whereabouts of the victim need not be informed to anyone if she and her children are in a temporary shelter for safety from the abuser. If the matter is leaked out to others the abuser may get the information and can have an opportunity for further and more aggressive attacks on his wife and children. This will lead to the next phase of abuse.

The clergy should not be the decision maker for the abused women, but can give valid Biblical counseling, up to date information, encouragement and alternate suggestions or arrangements.

The victim must be aware of the Biblical principles. The victim needs to explicitly deal with the individual wrongdoing or misbehavior. In Matthew 7:3-5, Jesus rebuked the hypocritical way of thinking and judging others by using 'speck of sawdust' and 'plank'. Before we judge others, take time to evaluate ourselves. I John 1:9, there are two important words 'faithful and just.' but basically one single concept which signifies that God answers those who confess their sins. The victim needs to truthfully and fearfully face the transgression of others. The abuser needs to repent. According to King Solomon, "He who conceals his sins does not prosper, but whoever confesses and renounces them finds mercy." (Proverbs 28:13). The joy of the forgiveness must be emphasized (Psalm 32:5, 10-11). Never allow the abuser to make lame excuses for his actions. He must repent before God, and then to the victim not only for his sinful behavior and dealings, but also for the wicked attitudes and beliefs behind the actions of abuse (Psalm 51; Romans. 12:19).

Guide and counsel the victim to tactfully deal with the abuser when it is appropriate and feasible. In the gospel of Mathew 18:15 we read, "If your brother sins against you, go and show him his fault, just between the two of you. If he listens to you, you have won your brother over." In this way she protects the abuser from the harm of further scandal. According to Luke 17:3, "...if your brother sins, rebuke him, and if he repents, forgive him." Never talk about the incident after one has forgiven the abuser. This will not give inner healing. Victims of abuse can turn out to be overcomers, by God's marvelous grace. Romans 12:21, "...overcome evil with good." Guide them to the Biblical promise of eternal hope and comfort. Romans 15:4, "...through endurance and the encouragement of the scriptures we might have hoped." The Apostle Paul is saying the purpose of scripture is for our instruction, so that we may patiently endure and hold fast hope in Christ. Teach the victim the Biblical view of pain and suffering. II Cor. 4:17 assures that eternal glory is greater than all the suffering one may face in this world. Therefore one needs to face pain and suffering of all sorts with the help of our master and Saviour Jesus Christ. Assure the victim with the Biblical promise of 'God's sovereignty' over all their suffering. God is in control of every situation. The Apostle Paul in Ephesians 1:11 say that Christ is the center of all God's plan in our lives. The close affiliation with Christ leads to a meaningful prospect.

Mahatma Gandhi, the father of our nation said that the weak can never forgive. Forgiveness is the attribute of the strong. It is true indeed; forgiveness is a quality of a strong personality whose trust is in the Lord rather than a coward or a weak individual. Claire Frazier,[6] says "When we forgive, we free ourselves from the bitter tie that binds us to the one who hurts us." From the above two statements it is clear that forgiveness is not an easy task but it is an attitudinal changes in an individual for a healthy and long-lasting healing relationship. In the book 'Forgive and Love again: Healing Wounded Relationships' John and Thomas state "Four stages of forgiveness which are face the offense, feel the offense, forgive the offender and find oneness-if appropriate."[7] The above mentioned four stages in the process of forgiveness are self descriptive. It is a process of renewing our mind day by day. Both the abuser and victim have a great role in the ministry of forgiveness. The element of forgiveness is not a human quality or character but it is a divine action and intervention. Therefore forgiveness is to remove all resentment against the abuser and love him with love like Christ's towards the church. This is the agape love mentioned in John 3:16. Firstly, face the offense honestly, bravely, courageously and with all humility. Avoid all lame excuses. Secondly, feel the offense. Feel it genuinely with full reality. Remove the mask from every aspects of your life. Accept the pain as it is and do not cover up the pain and agony in life. Thirdly, be willing to forgive the offender unconditionally. Never carry an unforgiving spirit in your life all the time. In every reconciliation there should be transparency in dealings and changes in behaviour and attitude. To reconcile the abusive situation both the abuser and victim need to be mentally prepared, willing to change and accept the reality, forget the past and look for a brighter future but more so make Christ as the head of the family. All decisions shall be made together and placed in front of God for his guidance and leading. Thus the fights and disputes could be reduced.

Many questions may arise at this juncture. Who should initiate forgiveness? When to forgive an abuser? Which are the areas the abusers need to be forgiven? How far to be forgiven? How should a victim forgive an abuser without any reservation? How much time to be given? Should they involve any mediator? Who can convince them of the uniqueness and the effect of genuine repentance? Where there is true repentance, there is a Godly sorrow behind it. Godly sorrow means a sorrow that comes from the bottom of the heart and not merely by saying, 'I am sorry' through lip service. II Corinthians

7:10, "Godly sorrow brings repentance that leads to salvation and he leaves no regret, but worldly sorrow brings death." At times we can notice instant and unrealistic sorrow among abusers. Godly sorrow is very different. The abuser must weep and plead before God and say goodbye to all their inhuman behavior. In other words, he must say 'no' to all his earlier behaviour and never repeat it and must accept a new way of life. He must seek forgiveness from all those whom he ill-treated (Matthew 5:23-24).

Forgiveness is not a theoretical approach, but practical, because Christ has forgiven each one of us. Teach the victim the Jesus' method of forgiveness. Jesus said in Matthew 6:12, "Forgive us our debts… have forgiven our debtors." Apostle Paul in Ephesians 4:32 says, "Be kind and compassionate to one another, forgiving each other, just as in Christ God forgave you." Forgiveness is a mind-set of Christ. Therefore the followers of Christ must follow the attitude of Christ for healing relationships. We received forgiveness for our sins; Christ showed us kindness and compassion even when we were sinners. Still he shows the forgiving spirit, kindness and compassion in our day to day lives.

Teach the abuser to practice servanthood, as Christ demonstrated to us. The life of God's children is characterized by humility, loving concern, and loving service (Mark 10:42-45, John 13:1-17). Jesus Christ transforms the sinners into saints. In II Corinthians 5:17, "Therefore, if anyone is in Christ, he is a new creation; the old has gone, the new has come." Everything can be possible through Christ's marvelous grace. A true and genuine confession is essential for a smooth relationship. II Peter 1:3 gives us the promise that a legitimate reverence towards the Almighty will oversee our attitude and behavior in every walk of life.

Take quality time in counseling the victim and the abuser. Bring to their minds the marvelous lesson from the life of Joseph from the Old Testament (Genesis 50:17-21). He was physically, socially and psychologically abused by his brothers. Joseph, a wise and upright man, forgave his brothers who did evil to him willfully and sold him to slavery. But God blessed Joseph; he was second in command to the mighty 'Pharaoh' of Egypt. When there was a great famine in all the land, his brothers came to him for shelter and mercy. Joseph had ample opportunity to take revenge on them but Joseph chose to forgive them and won their hearts through patience. (Genesis 45:5-8). He had the surety of control and the righteousness of God, even though many adversities happened to him (Genesis 50:20 41:51). He refrained from taking vengeance against his family members, and completely surrendered everything to Almighty God by trusting him to handle the whole situation and those who mistreated him (Genesis 50:19; Romans 12:19; I Peter 2:23). He was gifted with plenty of grace from God enough to forgive and bless his abused brothers (Genesis 50:21 Romans 12:20-21). This is an amazing model even today and the time to come, especially in the situation of abuse and crisis situations.

Meet the abuser personally and listen to his viewpoint in an unbiased manner, find out the reasons that made him abuse his wife. It is imperative to deal with the attitude of the heart behind the abusive behavior. Change of heart is more important than anything else (Mark 7:20-23). Usually the abuser doesn't get what he wants, and then he is prone to get angry and develop abusive behaviour (James. 1:19-20). Some of the general characteristics of the abusers are as follows - controlling and manipulative, blaming others and minimizing his own shortcoming, impulsive and aggressive, impatient during the times of stress, self- centered most of the time, and dishonest. Abusers tend to follow a vicious cycle of abuse. Firstly, tension building, secondly, battering with verbal or physical abuse, asking for forgiveness and lastly, again tension building.

Use the scripture as a changing agent in his life rather than any psychological or philosophical approach or teaching. Teach him about anger management. Anger is an emotional feeling, an effective psychological and sociological instrument to wrestle with the injustice and evil in the society in which one lives. Unrestrained anger can often lead to harmful and dangerous consequences. The apostle Paul in Ephesians 4:26 give the exhortation that Christians should not lose their temper in an unhealthy manner and their emotion should be controlled all the time. Psalm 4:4 says, "in your anger do not sin; when you are on your beds, search your hearts and be silent." Uncontrolled anger led to the first murder in Genesis 4:3-8, the killing of Abel by his own brother, Cain.

Permitting anger in one's life means to persist in the heart to give way to evil desires or give an opportunity for Satan to mismanage all affairs. Human anger cannot achieve God's righteousness and blessings, and human anger destroys all good and healthy relationships. The best way to control one's anger is to ask God's guidance and help by trusting him completely. King Solomon gives a promise in Proverb 3:5,6 "Trust in the Lord with all your heart and lean not on your own understanding; in all your ways acknowledge him, and He will make your paths straight." By trusting and acknowledging God and serving him with a faithful heart, he will remove the obstacles from your path.

The following are some of the causes for emotional outbreak: disagreement, experiencing pain for a long time, inner hurts, lostness, misunderstanding, stress, strain and anxiety and keeping feelings bottled up inside for a long period of time. King Solomon in Proverbs 25:28, "Like a city whose walls are broken down is a man who lacks self-control." Self control is a key factor in every tension building situation. If a man can control the situation then he will be able to handle the situation effectively. Lack of self- control means he is a defenseless person. Teach him how to control or overcome anger during the normal or tension time in life. Take time to ask, 'Is my anger reasonable or justifiable'? Admit the responsibility of the behaviour when you are angry, and accept some situation as beyond your control.

Temptation comes to us in many ways and forms. Over and over again we think of being tempted as being enticed to steal, murder or committing adultery. But time and again we are tempted to be impatient, miserly, envious, annoyed, covetous or any number of other things that we consider as lesser sins. Satan always strikes at our point of weakness. He knows exactly how, when, and where to strike. "Blessed is the man who perseveres under trial because when he has stood the test, he will receive the crown of life that God has promised to those who love Him" (James 1:12). Overcoming temptation is a skill that every follower of Christ will need to learn. It is fundamental to break sexual addiction and to successfully live for God. If the abuser can take time to understand the various temptations which he faces in his life, the clergy can help him.

Persuade the abuser of the wrongness of abuse, explain it politely and request him to make the necessary changes for a better, joyful, meaningful, and lasting marital relationship. He must be given ample time for change. Change is a process.

The need for financial autonomy, safety measures, education and job placement should be thought about seriously so that the woman is empowered to stand on her own feet, facing the situation boldly, taking care of the children and becoming spiritually strong.

Make the abuser aware of the existing laws against the abuse of women, which include severe punishments and also make him understand that abusing women is a crime and a sin in the sight of God. He should be made aware of the seriousness of abuse of women and the consequence of such a painful experience and the guilt feelings in the life of both husband and wife.

Give the abuser sufficient time to think, change and act. Meet with him often and assist him examining his positive or negative reaction to correction through the counseling. If there are no positive changes, refer him to a professional counselor.

If the response from the husband is positive, call the husband and wife for a combined counseling session. Counseling the couple can be initiated once the violence has slowed down. In joint counseling, both parties need the freedom to express their concerns honestly and openly without further arguments.

Encourage the couple to attend retreats, seminars or any spiritual family enrichment programmes which will help them to live a life which is pleasing and glorifying God. Introduce them to Bible study groups and invite them for cottage prayer meetings regularly.

Make sure that elders, committee members and clergy find time to visit the house and spend quality time, and some time in prayer with the family. Always make sure their visit will not aggregate any unhealthy situation. These visits should be spiritually oriented.

Role of Church

Most church leaders and congregation are uncomfortable and very sensitive when it comes to talking about the issue of abuse. They feel that if the issue of abuse is brought to the limelight it can lead to strained inter-personal relationship between the clergy, congregation, victim and victimizer.

Nevertheless the church and the clergy should have the courage not to follow the customary beliefs which lead to abuse. Each member of the church should be an agent of change, and should change the church and the community rather than being changed by the world around them.

Most of the married women were keen that the church committee should strongly condemn the wrong doings of the parish members. Clergy should maintain an impartial attitude towards the rich and poor in his congregation. He should give special attention to the most vulnerable group. He must recognize and execute his responsibility to be a good shepherd.

If the husband is unwilling to listen, then call him before the church committee and warn him. If he is not willing to listen even to the church committee, then withdraw his active church membership and do not permit him to serve in church committees until there is a positive and healthy change in his marital relationship.

The need for financial independence and security for women should be considered. Education and job placement for women should be assisted and encouraged by the church and the clergy. She must be empowered to stand on her feet, facing the reality boldly, taking care of the children and becoming strong in the Lord. In I Samuel 30:6, "... David found strength in the Lord his God" when he faced problems in his life. Nehemiah 8:10, "...the joy of the Lord is my strength." According to Apostle Paul in Philippians 4:4, "Rejoice in the Lord always. I will say it again: Rejoice!"

In a few denominations the participation of women in church administration and committees are limited. Clergy should ensure that there is an increase in participation of women in the church activities. The clergy should condemn the wrong deeds of the parish members; lovingly rebuke the abuser irrespective of his status or influence in church or society.

They should develop strategic plans to prevent abuse of women in Christian families. Value based education should be provided from childhood through Sunday school. Men and women are equal in the sight of God. This biblical view should be imparted from childhood itself. This shows the necessity of having Sunday schools and programmes for youth and young adults.

Another important step is to arrange women's fellowship, retreats and Bible studies in a regular manner. Women's groups allow them an opportunity to express their views without much fear, arguments or reservation as they find it easy to communicate with those of the same gender. The group should feel strong enough to tackle women's issues in unison and should be a friend to the women in difficulty. They can tell the abuser, without provoking him in any manner, that what he is doing a wrong. They can seek adequate help from various women cells, and direct them to a good counselling centre if necessary. Their home can be offered as a temporary place of shelter for women and children if an emergency arises. The victim may feel unsafe, insecure and uncomfortable attending church services if her partner is present for the service or comes to know she is attending the service. Therefore the women's group can direct and make her comfortable by encouraging her to attend the service, bible study or fellowship groups.

Jesus' interaction or communication with women gives a clear picture on gender equality. Jesus never degraded the women in his life and ministry. He respected them as human being. The women were the co-workers with him.

The Semitic and Greco-roman perspective saw women as subordinate to men. Jesus respected women, speaking to them as individuals with worth and value, with spiritual understanding. Jesus treated women as intelligent, thinking humans, equal with men. His attitude for women was remarkable in a day when men thought women were a grade lower than themselves. He drew out her knowledge, listened to her, and led her on to reach her own conclusions. He did not impose his rules on her. Instead, Jesus saw her, a woman, as having wisdom. He included them in his ministry on earth, they followed him to Calvary on the day of crucifixion and he appeared first to them on the day of resurrection. While they were victimized, he not only defended them but also challenged the injustice against them (John 8, Luke 7). Revealing his Messiahship to women (cf. John 4, 11) and making them the first announcers of his resurrected new life (John 20), Jesus entrusted women with his mission making them partners in the realization of God's dream for humankind. These outlines can be utilized for preparing regular Bible study classes for men.

Another important aspect to be taught to the congregation is about dowry. Though it is not done publically, demanding dowry in cash or kind and making further demands should not be done. 'Giving dowry and taking dowry' is punishable by the law. It is a social evil, which breaks up our family ties and healthy relationship at home, church, society and nation. The dowry Prohibition Act must be fully implemented for the desired results. Serious action must be taken against the families as they are involved in dowry demand, abuse or harassment. We live in a society where corruption, dishonesty, prejudice and biased dealings still exist. A special court could be established to hear dowry harassment cases so that judgment can be pronounced as fast as possible without any dely. "The number of functional family courts in India was 439 as of May 2016. The top 10 States in terms of the number of functional family courts were: Uttar Pradesh, Madhya Pradesh, Bihar, Kerala, Rajasthan, Karnataka, Maharashtra, Jharkhand,

Chhattisgarh and Tamil Nadu as of May 2016."[8] These courts are filled with registered cases. A Gender neutral magistrate must be appointed to give the final verdict.

The church leaders must develop good rapport with government authorities, Women's groups and NGO's so that quick consultation and help can be sought. Volunteer to assist and participate in 'prevention of abuse' campaign organized by these groups. Explore the possibility of developing and franchising social free enterprise models to reduce or eliminate the abuse of women.

In every police station there must be an unbiased and uncorrupt police officer who is trained to handle or assist the victims with proper care, sympathy and maintain decency and empathy. Appropriate training must be given to the police to handle domestic abuse cases. Be more practical and seize advocacy opportunities to advocate on issues that are central to women's interests. As per the instances quoted by the media, many deaths are relegated as suicide rather than natural deaths, whereas the causes are due to different forms of abuse. This is always covered under the umbrella of law. Therefore there is a need for transparent police officers in police stations to take on cases against dowry harassment. The law must be strict to take stern action against the police officers who refuse to register FIR (First Information Report) of the victims. Unfortunately many police stations are unwilling to register the FIR due to unnecessary involvement of political or spiritual leadership.

Empowerment

The clergy have a great responsibility and accountability to empower women in their church. They should be sufficiently prepared to resist and to react against abuse in a healthy and godly manner. The concern of clergy is to make sure the safety and security of the victim and her children with the help of church committee and volunteers from the church. The clergy should affectionately admonish the abuser irrespective of his position in church or society. The clergy should follow the principle of "...speak the truth in love" (Matthew 18:15-

20), provides a model for confronting an 'abuser' within the church. According to verse 17, the basis for excommunication from the fellowship is when an individual refuses to act in response to church discipline. Probably this is difficult in the modern world. In 2 Timothy 3:16, the apostle Paul provides a model for teaching, rebuking, correcting and training in righteousness.

Even though only a few victims in the survey reported that they had approached clergy for help, the majority of the respondents think that the church and the clergy have an enormous responsibility in cracking down on the abuse of women. Some clergy play a safe game by not taking any active steps even when these issues are shared with them. Very conveniently they say, 'let us pray about it', 'your suffering is much less compared to what Jesus suffered on the cross', 'wait for the day when you see changes in your husband', 'spend more time in prayer and meditation', and finally to 'adjust'. None of these statements can bring any comfort or solution to the one who is abused. She will feel ashamed of herself for approaching the clergy.

A few respondents said that they have heard from their parents or elders about the clergy of olden days who competently solved the family problems by their authoritarian style or their love and concern for the family members or their commitment to the Lord through serving humanity and using the wisdom God has given. They visited the families regularly and had a rapport with them; they insisted on family prayers, emphasized God's word and disciplined the wrong doers with authority. Some women said that this is possible even in this era.

Few church denominations teach that women should be quiet and submissive before men. One elderly woman, who has a purist ideology, said that she is suffering as Christ suffered. Her beliefs have a wrong concept. Another respondent said that she will have a greater reward in heaven if she suffered in this earth, so she suffers the abuse from her husband silently as she longs for that great reward. This is an old concept that women should suffer abuse from their husbands, thus becoming living sacrifices. This does not have any Biblical relevance.

The woman must understand that she is in no way subordinate to her husband. She must also make the husband aware of his fault in abusing her. This emphasizes the need for strong preaching from the pulpit in the church. The clergy has to change its views on topics like the role of husband, wife, and the purpose of marriage.

The majority of the respondents said that women should never tolerate or yield to abuse. Women have equal rights; they should be respected and treated equally. All the potential and the qualities of a woman must be recognized and utilized to fulfill God's purpose.

Apprehensions and Unpreparedness of Clergy

In Indian culture, only certain issues are considered appropriate to deal with by the church. The reasons may be due to the church culture, ignorance of the church's role, and inadequate preparation of the clergy to deal with abuse.

Some pastor fear that lay people may turn against them if they try to introduce new ideas or talk about equality and mutuality between spouses. Also he feels that the older generation will be displeased if he does so.

Most of the church almanac is prepared and clergy are expected to deliver sermons accordingly. Although topics related to prevention of abuse can be incorporated with every sermon in a practical way, many do not attempt to do so as they have to please the church authority as well as the church leaders.

It was brought out during the interview that most of the clergy in the present scenario are neither carrying out their responsibilities nor fulfilling the expectations as in the past. They reiterated that the responsibilities of the clergy should be reviewed, modified and prioritized according to the modern era. They emphasized that the clergy should prioritize their activities, time and responsibilities so that they can fulfill the Great Commission of Christ (Matthew 28. 18:20, Luke 9. 1:6).

Today the church and its administration are often controlled by rich and influential parish members. As the church is focused on developing the infrastructure of parish, schools, hospitals, orphanages and related institutions and other developmental activities, clergy have to depend on wealthy and politically influential members of the parish. For their survival and extension of service, they need to maintain a rapport with them

Many families prefer to approach a professional counselor rather than sharing it with the clergy or the parish members for they fear gossip.

The clergy of eleven denominations both of rural and urban churches expressed in unison that they have great responsibility in reducing abuse of women. But due to time constraint, lack of skills and knowledge, lack of full co-operation from the family, relatives, church committee, or the church as a whole, they are unprepared to handle crisis situations in families. Constraint of time is due to various other activities and responsibilities, church administration and social work in addition to their own family responsibilities. The larger the parish, the less time is available for the clergy to spend quality time with church families. As a result the clergy are unable to maintain a close fellowship with the families in the parish, even though they desire to have closer fellowship. The pastor is often unaware of the problems faced in each family.

A few clergy said that they can preach on prevention of abuse against women but do not intend to get involved in counselling and they prefer to refer the women to appropriate agencies. Media report shocking news of clergy getting involved unnecessarily with women, abusing them in various ways, church and the law of the land taking action against them etc. This can adversely affect their family, ministry and church as a whole. Hence the clergy prefer to refrain from these sensitive issues.

These issues expressed by the clergy are matters of great concern and the church authorities must take a serious view on solving this.

Equipping the clergy, reducing their extra-ministerial jobs, continuing and in-service education must be considered.

Role of Theological Colleges and Seminaries

Theological colleges and seminaries in India are established to strengthen the churches by training, equipping and molding clergy, church and par- church leaders for preaching, teaching and healing, for ministry and mission by providing holistic, integrated education based on Biblical doctrines.

While preparing or revising the curriculum, it would be worthwhile to consult or include a few of the experienced clergy, Counselors, eminent leaders in the field of women empowerment, police officers and those NGO's working directly with abused women. Their experiences, challenges faced, remedial measures adopted and suggestions will be of great value. It must also be ensured that the curriculum prepared for theological students include the issues on abuse of women, social and ethical issues and the role of the church in preventing abuses. The teaching must be reinforced and emphasized with practical training in the ministry especially in the field of counselling.

The following are some suggestions for the subjects to be included in the curriculum of theological institutions-family counselling, pre-marital counselling, marital counselling, women's empowerment, Christian Homes, Christian Family, raising the children, and Christian discipline, crisis management, conflict management, anger management, financial management, budgeting and other subjects. These subjects can be dealt with eminent teachers. Students must understand the need to update their knowledge through continuing education programme such as distance education, refreshment programmes and bridge courses. Exchanges programme with students from other countries should be welcome. The church must ensure that all clergy are sent for higher studies and provisions made to attend in-service and continuing education classes. Seminaries may develop an evaluation procedure to evaluate the clergy in a systematic manner periodically. This can be adopted by the church so that clergy can be assisted in many ways.

Scholarship must be arranged by the colleges to enable them to update themselves. Church or the local parish can also support them financially.

Endnotes

[1] Earl Canfort, "Is the pulpit a factor in Church Growth?" Bibliotheca Sacra, Vol.140.No:557, (January-March 1983), 67.

[2] D Martyn Lloyd Jones, Preaching and preachers. (Grand Rapids: Zondervan, 1971), 92.

[3] Ibid., 92.

[4] Thomas Varghese, By Grace to Graze-A walk through a Pastor's life (Delhi: ISPCK, 2015), 85.

[5] Ibid., 87.

[6] Claire Frazier served as a Special Education Teacher for the County Board of Education in Los Angeles, California.

[7] John Nieder & Thomas M. Thompson, Forgive & Love Again: Healing Wounded Relationships (Eugene, Oregon: Harvest house, 1991), 47-51.

[8] Functional Family Courts as of May 2016/open govt.trust data.http:// data. gov.in/catalogue/answer-data-rajya-sabha-session-239 Unstarred Question No: 1552. Number of family court (From: Ministry of Law and Justice).

Conclusion

Some people grumble that roses have thorns;
I am grateful that thorns have roses.

Alphonse Karr

When this study was initiated the author was not really aware of the extent and the different causes or forms of abuse experienced by women. It was an eye-opener as to how prevalent it is, even though many of us may not accept it as a reality. Many believe that this problem should not be brought to light and to make known to all especially to the non Christian community.

It turns out to be visible that a high proportion of Indian Christian women face different forms of abuse from their husbands, in – laws, immediate family members, neighbors and close friends. The extent of abuse varies from young woman to older woman, educated to uneducated, low to higher income level, religion to religion, culture to culture and rural to urban. In the olden days the abuse of women was also prevalent; however, it did not come to light as there were not much communication because of social, ethical or spiritual reasons. Even now only a low percentage of abuse is brought to the attention of the general public by the mainstream media. It is estimated that half of the incidences of abuse today are not reported due to the influence of family members, local leaders, politicians or church authorities.

Many people have an overall view that physical abuse is the only and major form of abuse that occurs in family life. It appears that most people think of physical bruises, cuts, and injuries while conceptualizing abuse. If injury marks are not seen in their body, people may not believe that abuse has taken place. The real fact is that majority of married women in urban and rural areas have experienced verbal, psychological, social and spiritual abuse from their husbands along with physical abuse. In addition, the respondents felt that with every forms of abuse they are psychologically affected, which does not heal completely and immediately. Some never reveal that they face abuse from their husbands due to the shame it could cause for their family, with loss of prestige and prominence in society. No doubt there can be differences in opinions in everything or in few things, but masculine force must not dominate and abuse must not take place.

Physical, financial and sexual abuse is greater among rural women than in urban areas. This may be due to a low educational, poor housing facilities, lack of adequate space to accommodate everyone in the house, irregular working hours, joint family system, lack of job opportunities and the financial dependency of wives on their husbands and family. Perhaps there is also a higher rate of substance abuse among these husbands, along with customs and practices which existed in their childhood. A woman mentioned during the conversation that due to custom and practices in her society, she saw her husband's face for the first time only after the marriage ceremony. This customs still exists in certain communities.

Husbands always give numerous reasons for abusing their wives. Some wives may have personality problems, are stubborn, disloyal, and disobedient and the list goes on. Though they think that the reasons mentioned are genuine, the author found out that some of them are mere excuses told to justify their actions. The reasons for which husbands abuse their wives can be either or both psychological, spiritual and financial. The psychological reasons include physical, emotional, financial and mental torture, misinterpreting views, unnecessary interference of family members or in-laws, doubts, and comparing his wife with other women with regards to dowry, physical appearance, smartness, finance and so on. The financial reasons include lower income, high expenditure over income, substance abuse, dowry, and the birth of a girl child. These all point to the fact that husbands think that they have the right to abuse their wives.

Abuse is primarily a closed door affair and in most cases there is no eye-witness or any genuine proof to support the arguments. For this reason, most people, especially clergy or church, do not want to get involved; there is lack of proper evidence. In this study the majority of married women said they suffer abuse behind closed doors, or they may be locked inside the room, at times abused when no one is at home, or they are alienated from public places. This fact should be seen as a serious matter because the abuse is most probably not known to outsiders or even to close family members. The wife is given threats by the abuser and thus she may never reveal the abuse. Even if family members are aware of this, they may either turn a blind eye or decide not to interfere. If a wife complains about abuse that has happened within closed doors, the husband can easily deny it as there is no proof. Moreover there is no one to stop the husband from abusing his wife if it happens behind closed doors, and she cannot even call for help even if violence against her is very unkind. Perhaps a husband abuses the wife behind closed doors because he is aware that abusing his wife is wrong and society will turn against him if it is known outside, and his reputation in the public-eye will be affected.

The women who felt ashamed to seek help said that their whole life or career would be ruined if the matter of abuse was shared with another person, either at her workplace, or the community where she lives. If it is known to others, getting good and promising marriage alliances for their children would also be difficult. Most of the time there is a tug of war in her mind whether to reveal the matter or not. While conducting the survey, five women had boldly taken a stand that they did not want their husbands to be 'put down' in front of others even though they are being abused frequently. They fear that this news of abuse would adversely affect the family reputation.

Most of the women did not seek help because of shame, or because they feared further abuse or threats. This was understood while analyzing the question, 'What are the reasons you are not seeking help during the abuse'? The main reason for the respondents who did not seek help was due to fear of intimidation and more harassment or unpleasantness from her husband. If she sought help to stop abuse, the husband threatened her with ruthless abuse or warned her of character assassination. The abusive behavior of some husbands sometimes includes attacking the reputation of his wife by saying his wife is a psychiatric patient, accuses her of having extra marital affairs or makes other derogative statements, in order to defend his own position and image. These allegations made by the husband are not always true. He blames his wife for his abusive nature. He also said that he will divorce her and she will be left with no financial support for her and the children. All these threatening factors help him to put his wife under his control without giving her any freedom.

The majority of rural women said that their families advised them to adjust with their husbands, whereas some urban women went to the extent of seeking advice for separation or divorce. Nowadays parents tell their daughters to come back home if any problems arise. Actually this kind of advice will give a signal to the children for separation or divorce; therefore they no longer try to prayerfully mend their broken relationship. In olden days the advice was different. The daughters were advised to adjust in her husband's home, not to share anything that is happening at his house, and to maintain the dignity of her husband, his family as well as her family. One can imagine why women suffered silently.

Religious teaching, cultural influences, and dependency made forty percentages of the respondents feel that they should tolerate the abuse from her husband, and there is no way out. So it is essential that this outlook should be changed. Day by day this outlook is changing at a fast pace. Nowadays many women are well educated, responsible, qualified, well placed and are financially stable. They are in position to handle the situation independently and are aware of their rights.

The major responsibilities of clergy are caring, teaching, preaching, counselling and shepherding the flock. One of the hurdles faced by clergy mentioned as insufficient training is a matter of great concern. Along with the clergy the church also has a role to play reducing abuse. The empowerment of women is an indispensable factor in this process. A healthy church should make use of the gifts and talents of every human being (male or female) for is glory and for the extension of is kingdom. The married women in the survey stated that the clergy must teach and preach from the pulpit regularly about preventing abuse. The women thought that an awareness of abuse from pulpit through the sermons could change the attitude and behavior of abusers.

God Restores a Broken Marriage

The Mathew 7:7b says "..seek and you will find." Seeking God constantly is very important. Before we seek we need to have faith in God. In Heb.11:1, "...faith is being sure of what we hope for and certain of what we do not see." Before seeking we need to hope for something which we cannot see. The assurance of things hoped for includes belief or faith in God- trust, reliance, and trustworthiness. Faith is the lifeline which connects to the Lord. If this lifeline is not active then you will lose your faith in the Lord, which leads to lose all contact with him. Then there is no hope for the reconciliation in any manner.

The Bible tells us that God wants us to 'grow' in his 'full knowledge' and 'grace'. And if you will be willing to grow in the knowledge of God through the study of scripture and through prayer life, then the Holy Spirit will start to increase your faith in the Lord.

If you are walking with the Lord, you must maintain a good, personal intimate relationship with him, and then the success in your prayer life is great and amazing. The apostle John says in John 15:7, "If you remain in me and my words remain in you, ask whatever you wish, and it will be given you." Therefore knowing him and believing his word are the sole criteria for answering our prayers. Then the Holy Spirit will help and guide you on how to become more sensitive to his leadings, his promptings, and his knowing what to do and how to do it.

You as the pastor, counselor, prayer warrior, or layman could cause some major changes and events in your church. There are different people who have powerful success in their prayer life. These are the kinds of people that you would want to team up with from time to time. These people are like the special forces of our spiritual military. These are the people that will not only get the job done, but they will get the job done in a very mighty and powerful way. Domestic violence is still present in church-going homes. Therefore the clergy, counselors, and lay leaders need view this issue with great importance, have better communication, deliver messages about prevention of abuse and, more generally on married life.

May a fire be lit in our souls to serve our community and uplift the hurt around us. Don't you see 'the bent women' around you, broken inside-physically, emotionally, socially, financially or spiritually abused, derided, bullied, beaten, deprived, miserable, thinking nothing of self? Can we be healing agents where women are hurt and catalyst for change where wrongs need to be corrected?

As I conclude, let me give all the glory, praise and blessings only to our Lord Almighty.

Bibliography

Abraham, Taisha. *Women and the Politics of Violence*. New Delhi: Shakti Books, 2002.

Ackerman, Nathan W. *Treating the troubled family*. New York: Basic Books, 1966.

Adams, Carol. *Woman Battering*. Philadelphia: Fortress, 1994.

Adams, Jay. E. *Shepherding God's Flock Volume 1-The pastoral life*. Michigan: Baker Book House, 1975.

Ady, Cecilia M. *Role of Women in the Church*. Westminster: Publication Board of Church Assembly, 1948.

Agrawal, C M. *Indian Woman*. Delhi: Indian Publishers Distributors, 2001.

Agrawal, Sushila. *Status of Women*. Jaipur: Prentice Publishers, 1988.

Ahuja, Ram. *Rights of Women: A Feminist Perspective*. Jaipur: Rawat Publications, 1992.

Al Miles, Rev. *Domestic Violence: What Every Pastor Needs to Know*. Philadelphia: Fortress, 2000.

Alvera, Mickelsen. *Women Authority and the Bible*. Illinois: Intervarsity Press, 1986.

Alsdurf, James, and Phyllis Alsdurf. *Battered into Submission: The Tragedy of Wife Abuse in the Christian Home*. UK: Intervarsity, 1989.

Antony, M J. *Women's Rights: Everything an Indian Woman Must Know About Her Rights - In Plain Language*. New Delhi: Dialogue Publication, 1985.

Archer, Gleason L. Jr. *Encyclopedia of Bible Difficulties*. Grand Rapids : Zondervan, 1982.

Arendt, Hannah. *On Violence*. New York: Harcourt Brace Jovanovich, 1970.

Armstrong, Alice. *Culture and Choice: Lessons from Survivors of Gender Violence in Zimbabwe*. Harare, Zimbabwe: Research Project, 1998.

Atkins, Anne. *Split Image: Male & Female After God's Likeness*. Grand Rapids: Eerdmans, 1987.

Atkinson, Sue. *Building Self-Esteem*. Mumbai: Better yourself Book, 2006.

Augsberger, D.W. Reconciliation :*The many faces of forgiveness. In conflict meditation Across Cultures: Pathways and Patterns*. Louisville: John Knox Press. 1992.

Bandura, V. *Agression: A social learning analysis*. New Jersey: Englewood Cliffs, Prentice Hall, 1977.

Beanmant, Paul R. *Christian perspective on Human Rights and legal philosophy*. UK: Paternoster Press, 1998.

Beck, James R and Craig L. Blomberg: *Two views on Women in Ministry*. Secunderabad: OM Books, 2002.

Bhasin, Kamla. *Understanding Gender*. New Delhi: Kali for Women, 2000.

Bhasin, Kamla. *What is Patriarchy?* New Delhi: Kali for Women, 1993.

Bhattacharya, Rinki. *Behind Closed Doors: Domestic Violence in India*. New Delhi: Sage Publications, 2004.

Bhuimali, Anil. *Education, Employment and Empowering Women*. New Delhi: Serials Publications, 2004.

Bishnoi, Anupama, Dahiya, Manju and Grover, Indu. *Empowerment of Women and Girl Child*. New Delhi: Anmol Publications, 2005.

Blumenthal, David R. *Facing the Abusing God: A Theology of Protest* .UK: John Knox Press, 1993.

Booth, A. *Men in families: When do they get involved? What difference does it make?* N.J: Lawrence Erlbaum Associates, Inc, 1998.

Bower, Robert. *Solving Problems in Marriage*. Grand Rapids: Eerdmans Publishing Co, 1972.

Brenner, Athalya. *Israelite Women: Social Role and Literary Type in Biblical Narrative*. Sheffield: J S O T Press, 1985.

Brenner, Athalya. *Feminist Companion to the Hebrew Bible in the New Testament*. Sheffield: Sheffield Academic Press, 1996.

Bristow, John Temple. *What Paul Really Said About Women* . San Francisco:Harper & Row, 1988.

Brown, Joanne Carlson, and Carole R. Bohn. *Christianity, Patriarchy, and Abuse: A Feminist Critique*. Ohio: The Pilgrim Press, 1989.

Brown, Robert McAfee. *Religion and Violence*. Philadelphia: Westminster press, 1987.

Bunch, Charlotte and Roxanne Carrillo. *Gender Violence: A Development and Human Rights Issue*. Dublin: Attic Press, 1992.

Bussert, Joy M. K. *Battered Women: From a Theology of Suffering to an Ethic of Empowerment*. New York: Lutheran Church in America, 1986.

Capps, Donald. *The Child's Song: The Religious Abuse of Children*. PA: John Knox Press, 1995.

Carol Adams. *Woman battering*. Philadelphia: Fortress, 1994.

Carroll, Wise. A,. The *meaning of Pastoral Care*. New York: Harper & Row Publishing, 1966.

Caron, Gerald. *Women on the Way with Jesus: Feminist Perspectives on the Bible and others*. [n.p]:Liturgical Press, 2000.

Churness, Vivian and Lisa R. Roberts, eds. *Midwifery for nurses in India*. Chennai: Ecumenical Books Services, 2018.

Clarke, Rita-Lou. *Pastoral Care of Battered Women*. Philadelphia: Westminster Press, 1986.

Conway, Helen. L. *Domestic Violence and the church*. UK: Patermoster, 1998.

Conway, Jim and Sally.*Women in middle crisis*. New York: Guideposts, 1971.

Cook, Kaye and Lance Lee. *Man and Woman, Alone and Together*. USA: Bridge Point Book, 1992.

Cunningham, Loren and David Joel Hamilton with Janice Rogers. *Why not women?* Seattle: Ymam Publishing, 2000.

Feldmeth, Joanne Ross, and Midge W. Finley. *We Weep For Ourselves and Our Children: A Christian Guide for Survivors of Childhood Sexual Abuse*. San Francisco: Harper, 1990.

Feliciano, David V. *On Male-Female Equality women, culture and revelation*. New Delhi: Regnum Asia Books,[n.d].

Fiorenza, Elisabeth Schussler & Copeland, Mary Shawn. *Violence Against Women*. New York: Orbis, 1994.

Flaherty, Sandra M. *Woman, Why Do You Weep? Spirituality for Survivors of Childhood Sexual Abuse*. [n.p]: Paulist Press, 1992.

Fortune, M.M. *Sexual violence: The unmentionable sin*. Ohio: The Pilgrim Press, 1983.

Fortune, M.M. *Violence in the family: A workshop curriculum for clergy and other helpers*. Ohio: The Pilgrim Press, 1991.

Fortune, Marie M. *Is Nothing Sacred? When Sex Invades the Pastoral Relationship*. San Francisco: Harper,1989.

Fortune, Marie M. *Keeping the Faith: Questions and Answers for the Abused Women*. San Francisco: Harper, 1987.

Fortune, Marie M, Rev. *Keeping the Faith: Guidance for Christian Women Facing Abuse*. San Francisco: Harper Collins, 1995.

Gaddis, Patricia Riddle. *Battered but Not Broken: Help for Abused Wives and Their Church Families* [n.p]: Judson Press, 1996.

Geisler, Norman L. *Christian Ethics: Options and Issues*. Grand Rapids : Baker Book House, 1989.

Groothuis, Rebecca Merrill. *Good News for Women: A Biblical Picture of Gender Equality*. Grand Rapids: Baker Books, 1997.

Grudem, Wayne. *Biblical foundation for manhood and womanhood-Foundation for family series*. Wheaton, Illinois: [n.pub], 2002.

Heggen, Carolyn Holderread. *Sexual Abuse in Christian Homes and Churches*.[n.p]: Herald Press,1993.

Horton, Anne L and Judith A Williamson (eds). *Abuse and Religion - When Praying Isn't Enough*. [n.p]: Lexington Books, 1988.

John, Susan. *Love Never Faileth: the Life and Times of Sister Anna Benjamin*. Tiruvalla: Christava Sahitya Samithy, 1996.

John, Mercy. K. *Dignity of women in Paul's letters*. Thiruvalla: Christava Sahitya Samithi, 2001.

Johnstone,Margaret Blair. *How to live every day of your life*. New York: The Bobbs-Merril Co, 1960.

Kivel, Paul. *Men's Work: How To Stop the Violence that Tears OurLives Apart*. New York: Ballentine Books, 1992.

Kivel, Paul. *I Can Make My World a Safer Place: A Kid's Book About Stopping Violence*. Almeda, CA: Hunter House Publishers, 2001.

Kroeger, Catherine Clark and James R. Beck. *Women Abuse and the Bible: How Scripture Can Be Used to Hurt or Heal*. Grand Rapids: Baker Book House, 1996.

Kroeger, Catherine Clark & Nason-Clark, Nancy. *No Place for Abuse: Biblical and Practical Resources to Counteract Domestic Violence*. Downers Grove: Intervarsity Press, 2001.

Leehan, J. *Pastoral care for survivors of family abuse: How to recognize and dealwith Long-term effects of physical and emotional abus*e. Louisville, Kentucky: Westminster/John Knox Press, 1989.

Lerner, Gerda. *The Creation of Patriarchy*. Oxford: Oxford University Press, 1986.

Lipman-Blumen, J. *Gender Roles and Power*. Upper Saddle River, New Jersey: Prentice Hall, 1987.

Livingston, D.J. *Healing violent men: A model for Christian communities*. Minneapolis: Fortress Press, 2002.

Loring, Marti Tamm. *Emotional Abuse*. New York: MacMillan,1994.

Lush, Jean. *Women and Stress-A Practical Approasch to Manging tension*. Secunderabad: OM Books, 1992.

McDill, S. R. and Linda McDill. *Shattered and Broken: Wife Abuse in the Christian Community - Guidelines for Hope and Healing*. [n.p]: Fleming H. Revell Co, 1991.

Mc Rae, William J. *Preparing for your marriage*. Grand Rapids: Zondervan Publishing House, 1908.

Menon, Latika (ed). *Women Empowerment & Challenge of Chang*e. New Delhi: Kanishka Publishers, Distributors, 1998.

Mickelsen, Alvera. *Women Authority and the Bible*. Illinois: Intervarsity Press, 1986.

Miller, M.S. *No Visible Wounds: Identifying Non-Physical Abuse of Women by their Men*. New York: Fawcett Columbine, 1995.

Mohindra, K.S. *Women's Health and Poverty Alleviation in India*. New Delhi: Academic Foundation. 2009.

Murphy, Nancy. *God's reconciling Love: A Pastor's handbook on Domestic Violence*. Seattle, Washington: Faith Trust Institute, 2003.

Myhand, M. Well & Kivel, Paul. *Young Women's Lives: Building Self-Awareness for Life*.[n.p]: Hunter House Publishers, 2001.

Otwell, John H. And Sarah Laughed: *The Status of Woman in the Old Testament*. Philadelphia: Westminster Press, 1977.

Owens, Virginia Stem. A *feast of families*. Michigan: Zondervan Publishing House, 1983.

Patterson, Gillian. *Still Flowing: Women, God and Church*. Geneva: World Council of Churches Publications, 1999.

Peace, Martha. *The Excellent Wife: A Biblical Perspective*. Minnesota: Focus Publishing, 1977.

Pence, E and Paymar, M. *Education groups for men who batter. The Duluth Model*. New York: [n.pub],1993.

Pierson, Anne. *Mending hearts mending lives-a guide to extended family living*. Pasadena:Destiny Image Publishers, 1987.

Poling, James N. The Abuse of Power: A Theological Problem. Nashville: Abingdon Press, 1991.

Rabey, Lois Mowday. *The Snare-Undersatnading emotional and sexual entanglements*. Colorado: Navpress, 1988.

Rebecca Merrill Groothuis. *Good News for women: A Biblical picture of Gender Equality*. Grand Rapids; Baker Books, 1997

Ries, Sharon. *To love and go on loving*. Eastbourne: Kingsway Publications, 1990.

Sahay,Sushama, *Women and empowerment-approaches and strategies*. Delhi: Discovering Publishing House, 1998.

Saxena, Shobha. *Crimes Against Women and Protective Laws*. New Delhi: Deep and Deep, 1995.

Shanthi, K (ed).*Empowerment of Women*. New Delhi: Anmol Publications, 1998.

Siddons, Philip. *Speaking Out for Women: A Biblical View*. Valley Forge: Judson Press, 1980.

Sider, Ronald.J.*Christ and violence*.Scottdale:Herald press, 1979.

Smith, Lynn. *Women, Worth & Scripture*. Bangalore: SAIACS Press, 1988.

Sonkin, Daniel Jay. *Domestic Violence on Trial: Legal Dimensions of Family Violence*. New York: Springer Publishing, 1987.

Stagg, Evelyn and Stagg, Frank. *Woman in the World of Jesus*. Philadelphia: Westminster Press, 1978.

Stewart, Charles William.*The Minister as Marriage Counselor*.New York:Abingdom Press, 1961.

Swidler, Leonard. *Biblical Affirmation of Woman*. Philadelphia: Westminster Press, 1979.

Swindoll, Chuck.*The Strong Family-Growing wise in family life*.California:Insight For living,1988.

Terrien, Samuel. *Till the Heart Sings: a Biblical Theology of Manhood and Womanhood*. Philadelphia: Fortress Press, 1985.

Thornton, Edward.E. *Theology and Pastoral Counseling*.Philadephia:Fortress Press, 1964.

Tracy, Steven. *Mending the Soul: Understanding and Healing Abuse*. Grand Rapids: Zondervan, 2005.

Trobisch, Walter. *Love yourself*. Germany: Trobisch, 1987.

Varghese, Thomas. *By Grace to Graze -A walk through a Pastor's life*. Delhi: ISPCK, 2015.

Varghese, Thomas. *Down the Aisle.* Delhi: ISPCK, 2017.

Walker, L. *The battered woman.* New York: Harper & Row Publishers, 1979.

Wise, Carroll, A. *The Meaning of Pastoral Care.* New York: Harper & Row Publishing, 1966.

Witherington, Ben. *Women in the Ministry of Jesus: A Study of Jesus' Attitudes to Women and Their Roles as Reflected in his Earthly Life.* London: Cambridge University Press, 1984.

Wood, Beulah R. *A casebook of Bible marriages.* Bangalore: SAIACS Publications, 2002.

Wood, Beulah R. *Protect yourself.* Secunderabad: OM Publication, 2004.

Wood, Beulah R. *Side by Side-Gender from a Christian Perspective.* Banaglore: SAIACS Press, 2007.

Worthington, Everett L. *Marriage Conflicts -Resources for strategic Pastoral Counseling.* Michigan: Baker Book House, 1994.

Wright, H. Norman. *A practical guide for pastors, counselors and friends – Crisis Counseling.* California: Regal books publishing, 1993.

Wyatt, John.*Matter of Life and Death.* England: Intervarsity Press, 1998.

Thesis / Dissertation

Alexander, P N. "Changing Pattern of Man and Woman Relationship in India and the Christian Witness in Relation to It." B.D. Thesis. Senate of Serampore College, 1967.

Anandaraj, Shanti. "Role of the Church towards the Deserted Women with Particular Reference to Abhayashrama" B.D. Thesis. Senate of Serampore College, 1990.

Anandraj, S D. "Women and Their Status in the Book of Proverbs." M.Th. Thesis. Senate of Serampore College., 2000.

Anderson, Elizabeth T. "Study of the Changing Role of Theologically Trained Women in the CSI since 1947." B.D. Thesis, Senate of Serampore College, 1986.

Anderson, Evangeline M K. "Comparative Study of Eve and Mary (Mother of Jesus) With Special Reference to Sin." B.D. Thesis, Senate of Serampore College, 1987.

Aniamma, P S. "Women's Perception of Counseling in Selected Pentecostal Churches in Adoor-Kottarakkara District, Kerala." M.Th. Thesis, Senate of Serampore College, 2000.

Arenla Ao, T. "Why Train Women? A Critical Analysis of the Role of Theologically Trained Women in Ministry in the Ao Baptist Church Association." M.Th. Thesis, TAFTEE, 2003.

Athyal, Leelamma. "Study on Ecumenical Discussion since 1948 on the Theology of the Role of Women in the Church." B.D. Thesis. Senate of Serampore College, 1978.

Dommati, Patrick. "Jesus' attitude towards the socially marginalized in the Gospel of Luke." M.Th.Thesis, SAIACS, 2006.

Yeoh Poh Choo, Monica. "Psycho-Social Problems of Filipino Maids in Kuala Lumpur: Implications for Pastoral Care and Counselling." M.Th. Thesis, Senate of Serampore College, 2002.

Electronic Sources

http//www.nfhs.org. (accessed 3 October 2008). National Family Health Survey (NFHS-3) Domestic Violence. 2005-2006.

http://www.doa.state.nc.us/doa/cfw "NC Council for Women and Domestic Violence Commission" "The Family Violence Prevention Fund" *http://www.fvpf.org (accessed 3 March 2006).*

http://www.thewordofhisgrace.org 2004.Joseph Arthungal "Grace for family life *(accessed 15 March 2006).*

http:// www.faithtrustinstitute.org-Faith Trust Institute -formerly Centre for the Prevention of sexual and Domestic Violence. *(accessed12 February 2006).*

Videos

Billie Sargent Hatchell, "Broken Vows: Religious Perspectives on Domestic Violence." Faith Trust Institute working together to end sexual and Domestic Violence. (1994). Part 2, 22 minutes.

Ann Downer, "Wings like a Dove: Healing for the Abused Christian Woman." Faith trust institute working **together to end sexual and Domestic Violence, (1997). 34 minutes.**